OTHER TEAM REAPER NOVELS

RELENTLESS

A TEAM REAPER THRILLER

BRENT TOWNS

WOLFPACK
PUBLISHING
— EST 2013 —

Relentless
A Team Reaper novel

Relentless is a work of fiction. Any references to historical events, real people or real places are used fictitiously. Other names, characters, places and events are products of the author's imagination, and any resemblance to actual events, places or persons, living or dead, is entirely coincidental.

Published in the United States by Wolfpack Publishing, Las Vegas.

Wolfpack Publishing
6032 Wheat Penny Avenue
Las Vegas, NV 89122

wolfpackpublishing.com

Paperback ISBN 978-1-64119-823-3
Ebook ISBN 978-1-64119-822-6

RELENTLESS

FROM THE CENTRAL
INTELLIGENCE AGENCY WORLD
FACT BOOK:

Italy: Important gateway for and consumer of Latin American cocaine and Southwest Asian heroin entering the European market; money laundering by organized crime and from smuggling.

Belgium: Growing producer of synthetic drugs and cannabis; transit point for US-bound ecstasy; source of precursor chemicals for South American cocaine processors; transshipment point for cocaine, heroin, hashish, and marijuana entering Western Europe; despite a strengthening of legislation, the country remains vulnerable to money laundering related to narcotics, automobiles, alcohol, and tobacco; significant domestic consumption of ecstasy.

Ukraine: Used as a transshipment point for opiates and other illicit drugs from Africa, Latin America, and Turkey to Europe and Russia.

CHAPTER 1

Team Reaper
Somalia

"Reaper One, you have two technicals inbound with what looks to be a bus following. Estimate they'll reach your position in three mikes."

John "Reaper" Kane, known so because of the large tattoo on his back, fired a single shot from his suppressed HK416 and saw another pirate fall. A hail of bullets rattled off the forty-four-gallon drum he was sheltering behind, forcing him to drop back down. "Copy, Bravo Three. We could use that air support about now."

"Roger. Latest intel has the two Super Hornets from the U.S.S. George Bush at least fifteen mikes out."

"Copy," Kane said, then muttered to himself, "I get it, we're fucked."

"Say again, Reaper One?"

"I said thanks."

"Sorry, Reaper. It's the best I can do."

More bullets ricocheted off the rusty drum, and Kane ducked lower almost laying his solid six-foot-four frame on the burning Somali sand. It was amazing how fast things had turned to shit. The op was meant to be simple. Go in, set the charges on the drug shipment, then get out. But things had gone sideways because of a mongrel dog that was hell-bent on biting Brick.

They'd inserted under cover of darkness, made their way by foot along the coast to the deep-water harbor of a small slum village, where their target vessel was. It was the rusted hulk of an old container ship which was being utilized as a drug storage facility. On the release of ransomed vessels, huge quantities of illicit substances were hidden aboard, to be collected at the destination by people on the payroll. The current intel had a substantial shipment being transferred to the *MSC Zoe,* which was a large vessel flagged in Panama, owned by a company in the U.S., now sitting in the turquoise water of the harbor, waiting to be liberated upon payment of fifty million U.S. dollars. The only problem was, there were no drugs and plenty of tangos.

Since being taken by the pirates twenty years before, and due to the shifting sands over that period, the storage ship that had once stood at anchor in the water, now sat derelict, mired in the sand.

"Reaper One? Reaper Two. Copy?"

Reaper Two was Kane's second in command, Cara Billings; a single mother in her mid-thirties, short dark hair, slim, and one hell of a team sniper. Who, at that moment, was on the bow of the hulk, providing overwatch armed with an M110A1.

"Copy, Reaper Two."

"Reaper, we've got three tangos circling around to the north of our position. Over."

"Roger. Can you see what they're up to?"

"Negative. They ducked around behind a shanty. Although I think one might have an RPG."

That's all we need. "Keep an eye out, Reaper Two."

"Copy."

Kane changed out an empty magazine and grabbed another from the webbing on his tactical vest. He slapped it home, loaded a round into the 416's breach and leaned around the drum just in time to shoot another advancing pirate.

Adjacent to his position, Brick was leaning across the rusted hood of an old Land Rover. He saw the tattooed ex-SEAL fire his carbine, his shaved head glimmering with perspiration in the heat haze as a new wave of bullets came hammering in, opening holes in the metal skin like an invisible can opener.

"How's your ammo, Brick?" Kane asked into his comms.

"I'm down to two mags plus what I've got for the M17."

The M17 to which he referred was the SIG M17, the team's handgun of choice. Kane said, "Reaper Two, Three, and Four, ammo sitrep."

"Two is good."

"Four is good."

"Three is down to two mags."

"OK. Conserve ammo. Only shoot at what you can hit," Kane ordered. "Reaper Four, shift position and move to Reaper Two. When the technicals come in, take them out."

"Copy. Reaper Four moving."

Reaper Four was Axe. Axel Burton, ex-recon marine and Team Reaper's second sniper when required. Otherwise, he just got down and dirty with the rest of them.

Carlos Arenas was Reaper Three. The ex-special forces commander from Mexico where he'd served for ten years, was in his late thirties. His hair was dark, and his jaw square, and his special forces background made him an asset to the team.

Again, more bullets rattled the drum as AK-47 rounds hammered into it. Kane spoke quickly into his comms, "Cara, I'm pinned down by the son of a bitch behind the stack of pallets to my ten o'clock."

"Copy, wait one."

A few heartbeats later, she came back. "Tango down."

Kane peered around the drum and saw the shooter, a man with skin the color of burnished copper, his clothes remnants of filthy rags, was lying in the sand beside the stack of pallets. The team leader nodded to himself and said, "Reaper One moving."

Traversing the gap to the Land Rover where Brick was sheltering, he made it safely and crouched down beside him. Brick looked at his team leader and said, "Holy shit, this is really fucked up, Reaper."

"Isn't it?"

"Reaper Four in position," Axe said as he took up his spot beside Cara on the bow of the run-down hulk.

"Copy, Reaper Four."

"Who do you suppose those fuckers are that're coming in with the technicals?" Brick asked.

Kane shrugged. "Could be anyone."

An accurate statement. It might be more pirates, al-Shabaab, or even al-Qa'ida. The known factor was that should they bring their heavy caliber weapons into the fight, then all kinds of shit would rain down, and a good chance that Team Reaper would be no more.

Kane rose and shot a wild-eyed Somali who was waving an AK around his head, encouraging others to push forward. The back of the man's head blew out in a spray of blood, and bone, and his knees buckled as his brain ceased all communication with the body's extremities.

"Reaper One? Zero. Copy?"

"Copy, Zero."

"I hate to tell you this, Reaper, but we just picked up a transmission calling for reinforcements, from your vicinity," Luis Ferrero, Team Reaper's operations leader said.

Kane's voice dripped with sarcasm. "Thanks for that snippet of good news, Zero."

"That is the good news, Reaper," Ferrero confirmed. "The bad news is we've just been informed that al-Qa'ida moved a terrorist training camp into that area about two weeks ago. Those technicals and the bus are the tip of the spear. We now estimate that you have around eighty fighting-aged males on their way to you as we speak."

Kane and Brick stared at one another, and the man everyone knew as the Reaper said, "Thank you very much."

————

U.S.S. George H. W. Bush
   Gulf of Aden
   12 Hours Earlier

Mary Thurston entered the briefing room, carrying a folder which she placed on the desk in front of her. The general was in her early forties, and her athletic build attested to her days as a Ranger. Her long dark hair was tied back, and she carried herself with an air of confidence.

Beside her was Luis Ferrero, also in his forties, but where

Thurston's background was military, Ferrero's was in law enforcement. The DEA to be exact.

Both had stern expressions on their face. Thurston was the overall commander of the Worldwide Drug Initiative, the official name of Team Reaper. Ferrero was in charge of field operations. Together they made a formidable team.

Before them in the gray-painted, drab-looking room sat every one of their charges—each with their own special job.

Kane, Cara Billings, Axe, Carlos Arenas, and Richard "Brick" Peters. They made up Team Reaper, with Brick a trained combat medic. Then there was the Bravo element. Brooke Reynolds, trained UAV pilot and sometimes field agent, with long dark hair and a tall, athletic build.

Pete Traynor; ex-DEA undercover, tattoos on his arms, unshaven, late thirties, and a good man to have in the field when required.

Pete Teller was the second Pete. He was an air force master sergeant who'd trained as a UAV tech. He, too, had served with distinction in the field.

And lastly, Sam "Slick" Swift, the team's computer tech. Capable of hacking anything electronic. If it was traceable, Slick could find it.

All together, they made one hell of a team in the fight against drugs.

"OK, listen up," Thurston began. "Tonight, you'll be inserted by a CV-22 onto the Somali coast."

The CV-22 was a variant of the V-22 Osprey Tiltrotor Aircraft that Special Operations used. It was equipped with extra fuel tanks and directional infrared countermeasures, as well as terrain-following radar.

A map on the bulkhead became visible to the team when Thurston stepped to one side. She pointed at the map and said, "Here's where it'll put down. And this is your target.

They're five klicks apart. You'll infil by foot to be in position well before dawn. You'll find the drugs aboard this old hulk." Thurston paused and pointed at a picture beside the map. "Once you locate them, plant the explosives and get out. Walk back to the LZ, and you'll be picked up from there."

"What's our alternate extract, Ma'am?" Kane asked.

"If you get into trouble and can't reach the extract point, there will be a SOC-R on standby to take you off the beach."

"Air support, Ma'am?" Axe asked.

Thurston nodded. "If you need it, you'll have it. The admiral has tasked a couple of Super Hornets to be placed on standby. Slick will also have a satellite tasked to keep an eye on things."

"Rules of engagement, Ma'am?" Cara asked the standard question.

"You stay in stealth mode all the way in and out. Unless it can't be helped. We estimate there to be approximately thirty hostiles on the ground. A firefight is the last thing you need."

Thurston went quiet, and Ferrero said, "Reaper, you've had a look over the intel. What do you propose?"

Kane leaned back in his chair and said, "Once we insert, we'll make our way to the target on the inland side of the dunes along the coast. On reaching the target, we'll take out any guards, and I'll have Cara and Axe set up overwatch on the hulk while Carlos, myself, and Brick go in and set the charges. Once that is done, we'll exfil towards our extraction point. Should anything go wrong while we're inside, Cara and Axe will be in a good position to hold off any tangos while we get the hell out of Dodge."

Thurston nodded her agreement. "Sounds good. Nice and simple."

"Nothing is ever that simple," Kane said, unaware of

how accurate those words would be. "What are the callsigns for the Hornets, Ma'am?"

Thurston checked her paperwork. "Callsign will be Rattler. Any other questions?"

Brick said, "Are there any HVTs on site?"

"Not that we're aware. The man in charge is low on the ladder. He just gets paid to hide the drugs on the liberated ships. We believe the real mastermind operates out of Belgium. Anything else?"

The room was silent.

"OK, then. Reaper, go over the plan with your people and then get some rest. You'll be wheels up at twenty-one hundred."

———

Team Reaper
Somalia

The insertion and the trek to the target area had gone off without a hitch. So too had the team's neutralization of the guards and placement of the explosives. The issue then was that they couldn't blow them immediately because Axe and Cara were still on the rusted hulk and the rest of the team were in the vicinity. Now it seemed like the whole world was starting to drop on them, and their only help was still a lifetime away.

"Reaper One? Reaper Two. Copy?"

"Copy."

"I've got eyes on the technicals. They're both white SUV trucks with what look to be fifty-caliber guns in the back. The bus is behind them is maybe five-hundred meters. It's a big bus."

"Roger. See if you can slow them down some."

"Will do."

Kane asked, "Bravo Three, copy?"

"Go ahead, Reaper One."

"Sitrep on the Hornets?"

"Still ten mikes, Reaper."

"Copy," a pause then, "Reaper Three, fall back on us, over."

"Roger. Moving now. Out."

"Reaper Four, cover Three from your position."

"I've got eyes on him, Reaper. He might need a path cleared for him."

"Then do it."

"Sending."

———

The M110A1 punched back into Axe's shoulder, and the 7.62 caliber bullet exploded from the barrel. It reached out the hundred or so meters and hammered into the naked chest of an AK-wielding pirate. No sooner had the man fallen when Axe said into his comms, "Reaper Three, move now. I'll keep their heads down."

"Roger that."

Through his scope, Axe saw Arenas break from the cover of an upturned dinghy which had offered him scant protection. As soon as the Mexican moved, the ex-recon marine shifted his aim and took down another pirate.

"Just like shooting fish in a barrel, huh, sweet cheeks?"

Cara never took her eye from the scope and said, "Call me sweet cheeks again, and I'll castrate you with my teeth."

The M110A1 fired again, and Axe said, "That sure sounds painful. Remind me to keep my mouth shut from now on."

Cara smiled. "Now that is something I would like to see."

"That is just downright nasty," the ex-recon marine said, feigning hurt feelings.

Another shot and Axe said into his comms, "You're clear, Reaper Three."

"Thanks."

Beside Axe, laying on the rusted deck, Cara was still monitoring the advancing technicals. She waited patiently, the crosshairs moving with the target. Breathing out slowly, she squeezed the trigger.

Through the scope, Cara saw the bullet strike. The head of the Somali at the fifty-caliber jerked violently, and she saw the spray of blood from the exit wound. His legs gave out, and he slumped into an untidy heap in the truck's bed. Then she shifted her aim and squeezed the trigger again. This time the front tire closest to her deflated catastrophically and the SUV swerved all over the dirt road before coming to a halt.

The other technical was about two hundred meters out and had to brake sharply and turn to avoid the one in front. The bus, in turn, took evasive action, flinging up more sand and dust into the already large plume created by the small convoy.

"Axe," Cara snapped. "See if you can take out the driver of the bus."

"Yes, Ma'am. Will do my best to see through the curtain of dust."

He shifted his aim and centered his crosshairs on the dust-laden window of the bouncing bus. He adjusted marginally and then fired. Axe saw the star pattern appear in the bus' windshield then it swerved violently to the right. It left the road and bounced through a ditch before coming to a stop in another cloud of thick orange dust.

Almost instantly, the bus doors flew open and armed men spilled outside. "Fuck," Axe snarled. "Get a look at these bastards. They're like fleas on a hound dog's ass."

Cara didn't respond because she had her own issue. Having already fired at the second technical's front tire, she'd missed, and the bullet had punched into the front guard instead. She took a second shot and cursed herself for rushing it and missing again. Then the SUV disappeared behind a shanty. She said into her comms, "Reaper One? Reaper Two. One technical is down but the second is on its way to you. Over."

"Copy."

Cara ducked her head as a burst of fire from an AK-47 blew rust chips from the edge of the bow no further than six feet from her face. Beside her, she heard Axe say something about an asshole before he fired two fast shots. Then he said into his mic, "Reaper, you've got company inbound. I would say at least fifteen jihadis from the bus. I stopped a couple of them, but they're swarming like flies on shit. They're amongst the shanties."

"Copy, Reaper Four. Just keep thinning them out."

"Roger that."

———

Kane shouted at Brick and Arenas, "Make sure the 416s are on single shot. Conserve ammunition and make them count."

Suddenly the second technical appeared. A man dressed in black was balanced behind the .50 caliber and no sooner had the vehicle stopped, he opened fire.

The Land Rover seemed to disintegrate around them as large caliber bullets passed through it like molten lances. What glass remained blew out, and Brick huddled in behind the engine block, figuring to use its solidity as extra protection.

Kane dived to his right while Arenas tried to make himself as flat as possible. The booming sound of the fifty seemed impossibly loud, and Kane shuddered from the concussive blast each time the weapon fired.

The 416 in his hands came up, and he fired three fast shots. Only one hit its target, but it was enough to do the job. The man fell back, and the fifty-caliber went quiet.

"Thank God for that," Brick cursed.

Kane nodded. "Reaper Two and Three. Keep an eye on that damned gun. Don't let them get it back up and running."

"Copy, Reaper."

"Reaper One? Bravo Three. We've got eyes on the rest of those jihadis coming your way. They are loaded in seven trucks. The good news is that there are no technicals. The bad news is that they'll be there before the Hornets."

"You're just full of good news."

Kane was about to say more when Cara's voice shouted over the comms, *"RPG! Reaper get out!"*

The three team members scrambled to get out of the immediate area. They hadn't gone far when the tell-tale smoke trail of the Rocket Propelled Grenade streaked through the air. The battered Land Rover exploded in an orange ball of flame, the heat wave washing over them all.

They were thrown to the ground by the concussive blast, and in the process, Kane received a mouthful of sand. His ears rang, and his vision blurred. Somewhere in the distance, the staccato sound of gunfire rang out. Then a voice which seemed miles away kept shouting at him.

"Reaper! Are you OK? Reaper, talk to me!"

He moaned and felt a tug at his clothing. "Come on, Reaper. Get the fuck up."

Kane coughed and spat sand from his mouth, the grains crunching between his teeth. He looked up and saw a figure swimming before his eyes. Slowly his focus returned. Brick took shape before him, a thin line of blood running from his hairline, and a bloody wound low down on his side beneath his tactical vest.

"Are you OK?" he managed.

"No worse off than you or Carlos," Brick told him. Then Kane realized that the burning pain in his thigh wasn't going away. He looked down and saw the bloody gash and the material around it covered in blood and sand.

"Where's Carlos?"

"I'm here, amigo," the Mexican said, and Kane saw that he too was wounded. On his upper left arm.

"Are you OK?"

Bullets hammered the ground around them. "How about we get out of here before we start taking inventory," Brick snapped.

Kane came to his feet and limped towards an old shed made from corrugated iron. The other two followed Brick covering their retreat. Bullets kicked up sand all around them, but Kane was hurting too much to care. They took shelter in the flimsy structure, rounds hammering into it sounding like a massive hailstorm.

"We have to get out of here," Kane shouted to the others.

The normally unflappable Arenas said, "No shit."

Kane coughed and winced. "That hurt."

Brick started to check him over. As he did, he said, "Carlos, look out the back. We need to get out of here before we get surrounded."

"Roger."

Arenas disappeared for a short time, and when he came back, said, "It is all clear."

Brick said to Kane, "I reckon you might have a cracked rib or two. And you might need a few stitches in that leg."

"Then I'll live?"

"I'd say so."

Kane said, "We need to get the hell out of here. Bravo Three? Reaper One. I need you to tell me what you see to our six, over."

"That's Indian country, Reaper One."

"I know that, damn it. But if we stay here any longer, we're all dead."

"Wait one."

"Cara, can you hear me?"

"Copy, Reaper."

"You and Axe rally on us. We're falling back."

"Into the slum?"

The slum he referred to was the corrugated iron dwellings which the pirates lived in while they were operational.

"Yes."

"Roger, coming to you."

"Everyone, check ammo," Kane ordered over his comms.

"Reaper One, your six is clear, over," Teller's voice came to him.

"Roger. Tell Zero we're falling back. How far out is that air support?"

"Hornets are still five mikes out. Listen Reaper; if you

go into the slum, there is no guarantee you're coming back out of there alive. It's like a maze, and with those truckloads of jihadis closing in on your position, it could all turn to shit."

"It already has. Reaper One out."

Cara and Axe appeared. "If we're doing this, Reaper, I suggest we go now. Those trucks are a minute or so out, and that fifty will be up –"

He never finished the words because the thump-thump-thump of the fifty-caliber machine gun beat him to it and large holes began to appear in the shed as though it was made of tin foil.

"Move!" Kane shouted. "Now!"

CHAPTER 2

U.S.S. George H. W. Bush
Gulf of Aden

Teller looked up at Ferrero in the makeshift operations room and said, "Did you get all that, sir?"

Ferrero nodded. "We need to get them some help, or it's all gone to hell, and we'll never get them back. I can't believe that we weren't told about the al-Qa'ida camp. Christ."

The watertight door opened, and Thurston appeared. "Sitrep, Luis."

"Kane is pulling them out, and they're withdrawing back into the slum," he told her. "I just hope they can hold out until air support gets there."

"I just talked to the admiral. He's having the marines spun up as a QRF. The problem is, they won't be on the ground for about forty minutes. What about the jihadis?"

Teller said, "They're almost on top of them, Ma'am."

"Shit."

Suddenly, Swift appeared beside them. "I might have something, Ma'am."

"What is it?"

"I've just been in contact with an Australian naval vessel, the H.M.A.S. Adelaide. She's up here on pirate patrol. She's been monitoring our radio transmissions, and they have a helicopter on standby with a SAS team on board. They informed me that they can have them on the ground within fifteen minutes."

Thurston glanced at Ferrero. "They're a lot closer than we are."

"I say do it. They're the team's only hope."

The general nodded. "Slick, tell them that all help would be received with our undying gratitude."

"Yes, Ma'am."

Ferrero said as he stared at the jihadis dismounting from their trucks, "I just hope they can get there quick enough."

Team Reaper
Somalia

"Reaper One, this is Rattler One-One. We are a flight of two, inbound your position, over."

Kane brought his team to a halt amongst the shanties and had them set up a small perimeter. He pressed his talk button and said, "Copy, Rattler One-One."

There was a loud boom as the afterburners on the two Super Hornets kicked in as they passed overhead. Reflexively the team ducked low. The lead pilot came back over the radio. "Both myself and Rattler Two-Two are armed with a pair of AGM-65 Mavericks. Where do you want us to put them? Over."

"Wait one, Rattler. Just stand off a moment, and we'll give you an aim point."

"Copy, Reaper One."

Kane turned to Brick. "Blow the damned drugs."

"Copy that."

Within seconds there was a roar, and the corrugated iron structures around them reverberated violently, threatening to fall on them from the blast wave as it funneled through the narrow alleys. An orange fireball rose above the small community and disappeared into a black pall of smoke. "You get that, Rattler One-One?"

"Yeah, roger. Can hardly miss it."

"Good. Anything within two-hundred yards of that damned explosion is fair game."

"Copy. Rattler One-One is inbound and cleared hot."

Cara said to Kane, "Just in case you missed it, we're inside that target area."

"Well, I guess we'd better move then," he said, pointing along an alley. "That way."

Cara took the lead and moved as fast as she dared. Suddenly a man appeared in front of her. This one, however, wasn't a pirate, but a jihadi. The thick beard, the lighter-colored skin, and better dressed. She snapped off a shot with her M110A1, and the 7.62 round slammed into his chest before he could fire his AK.

"Keep moving," Kane shouted at her and Cara did just that, stepping over the body and moving forward.

"Reaper One? Rattler One-One. Keep your heads down, missiles inbound."

Within a matter of moments, the first missile struck off to their right and rear. The impact was much bigger than that of the triggered explosion. The team dived to the ground where they remained for a handful of seconds before they were up and moving again.

But they'd progressed no further than another twenty meters when the second Hornet came in and delivered its payload. This time the two missiles landed closer than the others, and Kane's team was thrown to the ground rather than diving of their own accord.

Sand and debris rained down around them, pieces of corrugated iron forming deadly hail, and through the haze of it all, Kane heard the lead pilot say something about good luck, and then they were gone.

Slowly, painfully, the team dragged themselves to their feet, and battered and bruised, Kane got them moving again.

"Reaper One? Zero. Copy?"

"What?" he snapped, disregarding any kind of protocol.

Ferrero let it go and said, "How are you folks doing?"

"That last one was a bit close, but we're all still alive."

"Move to your west. Once you get out of the slum, you'll find a patch of broken ground with what looks to be a wash running through it. You need to get there in the next ten minutes."

"What's so time critical?"

"There's a chopper on the way in with a team of Australian SAS on it. They'll exfil you."

"Copy. We're moving. Out."

Team Reaper spent the next five minutes fighting their way through the slum against seemingly insurmountable odds, the tide of humanity multiplying the further they went. Suddenly the claustrophobic alleys opened before them in what resembled a town square. There were old boxes, a bathtub, and other various items strewn around. Kane cursed, and from behind him, he heard Brick say, "It's a fucking kill zone."

"Bravo Three, copy?"

"Roger."

"We've reached an open area in the middle of the slum which I'd rather not cross. Is there a way around?"

"Negative, Reaper."

"Shit. OK, Move out. The sooner we get across this, the better."

Arenas led the way with Cara behind him. Kane began to move out, followed by Axe, and Brick provided rear security. They were halfway across when the first jihadi appeared. He opened fire with his AK, spraying the clearing with a deadly hail of lead. The team scattered, trying to find cover. Kane dove behind a pile of crates which splintered under the impact of the incoming rounds.

Then, before that one could be dealt with, another appeared. And another, and another. Before long they were pinned down by a tremendous rate of incoming fire.

Kane leaned around the crates and rattled off a couple of shots, killing a jihadi. To his left, down behind the metal bathtub, Cara steadily fired at targets as they appeared. The others took up cover wherever they could, however meager it was. Cursing under his breath, Kane said into his comms, "Bravo Three, Reaper One. We're pinned down. I say again, we're pinned down and just about out of ammo."

"Copy, Reaper One. You're pinned down."

————

Aboard Dingo Four-One
    Somalia

· · ·

Warrant Officer Bluey Clarke looked over at his four team-mates, held up two fingers, and shouted, "Two minutes!"

Each man was armed with an M4A1 and had loaded up with extra ammo when the call came for them to deploy. Each man's vest had armor plate both back and front. Bluey had made sure of that before they'd climbed aboard the UH-60 Black Hawk helicopter. The information he'd been given before leaving the Adelaide wasn't much. All he knew was that a team of Yanks were in trouble and needed rescuing. His commanding officer had also told them that there would be plenty of rag heads to kill.

The team was very experienced and had been together for a while. Apart from himself, there was, Ringa, Jacko, Red, and Lofty; each man proficient at his job. They had to be. One slip could lead to death. Or worse, you could let your mates down.

Bluey pressed the talk button on the radio to speak with the pilot. "Can you take us in over the target first so I can get the lay of the land, Skipper?"

"Roger, Bluey. We're a minute and a half out."

"Can you give me an outside line, too?"

"Changing channel now. She's all yours."

"Bushranger One to American commander, come in, over."

Nothing.

"Bushranger One to American commander, come in, over."

There was another moment of silence before the radio crackled, and a voice could be heard to say, "Bushranger One, this is Reaper One, reading you Lima Charlie, over."

"Copy, Reaper One. We're inbound about a minute out.

The helo is going to do a sweep over the target before we land, over."

"Roger, Bushranger One. We're pinned down in the center of the slum and taking heavy fire, over."

"Hang in there, Reaper One. We'll be on the ground shortly. We'll come to you and exfil together. Bushranger One out."

The Black Hawk swept in over the slum, taking several incoming rounds from the ground as it did. Bluey leaned out the door to get a better picture of what was happening below. As they passed over the battle area where Team Reaper was pinned down, he saw the overwhelming number of jihadis pushing hard to close the circle and finish the infidels off.

Bluey said into the comms. "Skipper, when you drop us off, you might need to do a gun run or two over the target area."

The pilot said, "Leave it with me. We'll sort the bastards out."

The Black Hawk dropped close to the ground and flared before landing. Bluey and the others disembarked and crouched down, waiting for it to lift off and stop blowing the sand and shit in their faces.

Once it had cleared, Bluey signaled for his team to move out. Red took point and was followed by Jacko. Within moments, they were inside the alleys of the slum and moving toward the sound of gunfire.

Suddenly, the sky overhead seemed to be ripped apart as the minigun on the Black Hawk opened up. Invisible lances reached out, destroying all they touched. Bluey's team pushed forward and had only gone a few more meters when Red's voice came over the comms. "Contact front!"

The rattle of gunfire sounded as the point man opened fire. The rest of the team became backed up at a small crossroads within the slum and Bluey swore. A jihadi appeared to his right, and he swung his M4 around and fired. Squeezing his trigger, he called out, "Contact right!"

The shooter jerked violently under the impact of the rounds. Then Jacko called in contact left, and the SAS team were well and truly hip-deep in shit. "Motherfuckers," Bluey cursed. "Push forward, Red."

"Roger!" Red shouted and kept moving.

The battle raged as more attackers appeared, but the SAS team kept moving like a battering ram knocking down a stubborn door. Overhead the Black Hawk did another sweep, and the minigun rained devastation once more.

Bluey changed out a magazine and slapped another one home, chambered a round and brought the M4 back up into the firing position. "We're here, Bluey," Red's voice came over the comms.

"OK, hold your position," Bluey said and moved forward to Red.

When he reached him, he found his point-man sheltering behind a corrugated iron structure, with a dead jihadi at his feet. "What have we got?"

"It looks like they're pinned down in the center of the open area. There are shooters on three sides at this stage."

Bluey poked his head around the corner then ducked back. "Reaper One? Bushranger One. Copy?"

"Copy."

"We're coming in."

"Roger that."

"Dingo Four-One, come in."

"Got you, Bushranger."

"I need you to lay down fire to the north of the target area. Keep their heads down."

"Copy, Bushranger."

The Black Hawk came in over the target, and the minigun sprayed more hot lances. The iron structures of the slum were ripped apart under the torrent of lead. Bluey said, "Now!" into his comms and the SAS team broke cover.

On entering the exposed area, they fanned out, taking down targets of opportunity. Bluey directed Jacko and Red to move left. "Clear that side!"

The Australian took the others to clear the right. He noticed the Americans come to their feet and join the battle. With the two forces combined and the air support overhead, the attackers fell back, and the firing died away. Soon the only thing to be heard was the whop-whop-whop of the helicopter.

Bluey approached Kane who by this time looked more than a little worse for wear. He spoke loud enough to be heard over the Black Hawk, "Are you Reaper?"

Kane nodded. "Bushranger?"

"That's me, cobber. Gather your people together, and we'll get the hell out of here."

"Copy that. Glad to see you."

"Glad you're all still alive. Buy us a beer when we RTB."

"Roger that."

Bluey pressed his talk button and said, "Dingo One, this is Bushranger. We're moving to extract, over."

"Copy, Bushranger. See you on the ground."

Axe appeared beside Bluey, covered in grime and more than a few cuts and scratches. "Thank God for the Australians, huh?"

Bluey gave him a smile. "What the hell were you guys

doing in here anyway? Didn't you know about the al-Qa'ida camp?"

Cara stopped beside Axe. She looked just as bad except she had a bloody tear in her top just below her tactical vest, revealing a nasty-looking gash against a white background. "We were told," she allowed, "but it wasn't until after we were already engaged."

"Bugger."

"You've got that right."

"My people, move out!" Kane barked in frustration. Then into his comms asked, "Zero? Reaper One."

"Copy, Reaper One. Good to hear you."

"The cavalry has arrived, and we're heading to extract now."

"Copy. See you when you get back."

"You ready?" Bluey asked Kane.

"Yeah, more than ready."

The Australian pressed his talk button and said, "Jacko, on point. Let's go."

They walked towards the sound of the helicopter, past the fallen jihadis the Australians had killed on their way in. A few minutes later they broke out of the corrugated maze and into the open where the Black Hawk waited, and the crew chiefs stood guard with their own M4s.

Bluey pulled Kane aside and said, "You all get your asses on the bird. They'll take you to where you need to be."

Kane was confused. "What about you guys?"

The Australian gave him a big shit-eating grin and said, "We're going for a little walk. Check out that al-Qa'ida camp."

"Just the five of you?"

"Once they hear us Aussies are after them, they'll run away."

Kane held out his right hand. "Thanks for saving our asses."

Bluey took it in a firm grip. "Anytime. Keep your heads down."

"You too."

––––––

U.S.S. George H. W. Bush
Gulf of Aden

"That was a major fuck up, and you both know it! We were lucky to get out of there without losing anybody!" Kane seethed. He winced as the medical officer tended his ribs, having already put half a dozen stitches in his leg.

"I'd say you've got at least one that's busted, sir," the middle-aged man said, turning away to put down the tape he'd used on Kane's ribs.

Kane ignored him as he stared heatedly at his two commanding officers. "How the hell did we miss an al-Qa'ida training camp?"

"I don't know," Thurston said, her manner abrupt, letting him know she wasn't happy with the way he was speaking to her.

"Well, someone sure as shit should have."

"Reaper! Cool down," Ferrero cautioned him.

"The hell I will. We all nearly got killed today."

Thurston's eyes flared. "Enough! I'm sorry you all nearly got killed today, Gunnery Sergeant. And I'm sorry that the intel was all fucked up. But I won't have one of my subordinates speak to me that way. Do you understand?"

Kane glared at her defiantly.

"Do you understand?"

"Yes, Ma'am."

"Now, what's the report on your team?"

"Few cuts and bruises. Nothing a little rest and treatment won't fix."

"OK, when we get back home, everyone gets a week off to mend a little. Except for you. You get three weeks to let that rib heal."

Kane opened his mouth to voice his protest at what he figured was punishment for his insubordination, but Thurston was having none of it. "Not negotiable, Reaper. It's an order. Cara will be in charge while you're laid up."

"Yes, Ma'am. Is that all?"

"Yes."

Kane put on his shirt and left the room. Ferrero looked at Thurston. "He's pissed."

"And damn right he should be. That should never have happened. They were all lucky. She looked around the small gray-painted sickbay. "We could have been using this place to store bodies. From now on, I want all intel double-checked no matter the source."

"There was something else?"

"What?"

"Slick managed to track the drug shipment. Whoever is doing it has a set-up in the U.S. as well as Europe."

"Where in Europe?"

"Belgium."

———

Antwerp, Belgium

. . .

Middle-aged Dorian Janssen took the news about his lost drug shipment so well that he shot the man who'd delivered the news. He had obviously never heard the saying 'Don't Shoot the Messenger' and now stood over him, a Walther 9mm PPQ M2 in his hand, watching him bleed all over his five-thousand-dollar rug.

The door to his ornate library flew open, and a large man with a black beard entered, a gun in his hand. Janssen looked up and said, "Get this piece of shit out of my fucking sight, Sander."

Sander had once worked for the Belgian SFG – Special Forces Group – but private sector work paid better, namely Dorian Janssen, Belgium's richest drug supplier.

"Is there a problem, sir?" he asked in a deep voice.

The lined face darkened. "I lost ninety million dollars' worth of ecstasy in fucking Somalia. Someone found out about it and took it upon themselves to blow it up. At which time some al-Qa'ida assholes decided to make open warfare on them. It was just a complete shitstorm. Now I'm a shipment short and out all that money, not to mention down a supply route."

"Do you know who it was?"

Janssen shook his head. "I need to contact Dries and warn him. If they knew about the Somali part of the operation, then it's possible that they know about the other in America."

"What will you do now?"

"Back to the old routes. Through Europe, to Spain, then on to America, down through India then into the Philippines and Australia. It is more expensive that way, but what choice will I have? At least the Somalis did it for peanuts."

"Perhaps once things calm down, then you can open up the route again?"

Janssen grew angry again. "What I want to do is find out who leaked the information and kill them. See it done."

"Yes, sir."

With a scornful look on his face, Janssen indicated the corpse on his rug. "Right after you get rid of this."

CHAPTER 3

El Paso
Texas

Kane felt a hand on his shoulder and turned around on the barstool to see Cara grinning at him. "We thought we'd find you here. Drowning your sorrows ... again."

He looked past her at her companions; Brick, Arenas, and Axe. All were smiling as though they'd just received overwhelmingly-good news. "Pull up a stool, grab a beer."

With mock salutes, they did as he said and all ordered beers. The bar was relatively smoke-free, which was why the team frequented it. Sure, it was noisy and the music loud, not to mention the occasional fight, but hell, this was Texas. The beer was cold and the steaks at least an inch thick—all the comforts of home.

"What do I owe the pleasure?" Kane asked.

"We're leaving on a mission tomorrow," Cara told him.

"Where?"

"North Carolina. Wilmington. There's a warehouse at

the port, which we believe is tied to the drug smuggler in Belgium."

Kane asked the obvious question, "What is the intel like?"

"It's good. I checked it myself."

He nodded. At least they were being safe. Axe leaned forward onto the bar so he could see his friend past Arenas. "Don't worry, Reaper. Since you've been on holiday, she's been working the asses off us. I swear I'm running assault courses in my sleep."

Brick elbowed him. "There's only one thing you've been running in your sleep. What's her name? Elvira?"

Cara smiled. "That's her. The mistress of the dark."

The ex-SEAL snorted. "Mistress of the dark, bullshit. You need to move your bed away from the wall. Like right away. I swear, at the rate you two go at it, all that banging and screaming. If it keeps up, I might have to put a couple of 5.56 rounds through the damned thing."

"Bit of a screamer, is she?" Kane asked with a wry smile.

"Shit no, it's fucking Axe who makes all the noise."

Axe gave him an indignant look. "Now, why did you have to go and say that for?"

"Because it's true."

"Shit."

"Are we talking about the mistress of the night?"

The team turned and saw Thurston standing there with a smile on her face. Kane had to admit, dressed casual, hair down, his commanding officer wasn't half bad to look at. He nodded. "Yeah."

"Double shit," grumbled Axe.

"Get you a beer, Ma'am?" Brick asked.

She shook her head. "Thanks, no. I just came to see Reaper."

"Well, you found me."

The others moved along the bar to give them some privacy. "How are you doing, John? Ribs healing fine? Haven't seen you around."

"I'm OK."

"Did the others tell you we're leaving on a mission tomorrow?"

Kane drank the last of his beer and put the bottle on the bar in front of him, trying to remove the label. "Yeah, they did mention something like that."

"I want you to come with us."

"And do what exactly?"

"Run operations. Luis is sick, and I need someone I can trust to do it."

Concern flitted across Kane's eyes. "Is he OK?"

"He'll be fine. But like I said, I need you."

A waitress came down the bar and took Kane's empty bottle. Dressed in a white singlet top with cut-off jeans, she smiled at him. When she turned and walked away, he could see the wing tips of her angel tattoo, visible at the point of each shoulder. "Unless you've got something else, you'd rather be doing?"

For a moment, Kane thought about saying no, but these were his people, his responsibility. "All right. I'm in."

"Be at HQ by six-thirty in the morning," Thurston said. Then before she walked away from the bar, added, "She's not your type," nodding towards the tattooed waitress.

Kane stared after her and called out, "How do you know what my type is?"

Her only response was a wave.

———

Biggs Airfield
Outside El Paso

An F-15 thundered down a distant runway before picking up its nose and clawing its way into the clear Texas sky. Kane stood watching it go, a clipboard and pen in his hands. It quickly faded to a speck, and he turned and began to walk up the ramp of the HC-130.

Cara was coming the other way, and he asked her, "Do you have all you need?"

She was wearing jeans and a khaki T-shirt which hugged her form in all the right places. In a thigh holster, like the rest of the team, she had her SIG M17. With a nod, she said, "I think so."

"NVGs? Battery packs? Tac gear? Comms sets? Extra ammo? Spare weapons? Tac –"

"Yes," Cara said, cutting him off. "I've got this, Reaper."

Kane nodded. "Of course, you have. Listen, I've got intel and pictures for you to study on the way up. Work out a mission plan and let me know."

"You don't want to figure that one out?" she asked, surprised by his willingness to hand control to her.

"It's your team this time out. I'm sure you'll make good decisions."

Thurston approached the pair. "Have we got everything?"

Kane nodded. "Gear's all stowed, and everyone is on board."

"OK. Let's get this show on the road. Reaper, sit with me. I want to go over the intel we have."

"Roger that."

They all walked up the ramp and into the plane.

———

On Board
HC-130

Kane and Thurston wore headsets which enabled them to converse easier against the loud hum of the plane's engines. Thurston had satellite pictures and other written intel all in duplicate. The second set went to Cara, who was working on a plan of attack.

The general passed Kane a black and white picture which had been taken from a UAV. The warehouse was set back off the Wilmington port area with a large paved apron in front which catered to the size of the eighteen-wheelers that frequented it.

"That's the warehouse," she said. "There are two ways in and out. The DEA have had it under surveillance since we alerted them to it. At any one time, there are six or more guards. We've also received intel that there will be a shipment delivered tonight."

"So soon after we broke up their operation?"

"The Seattle Rover has come from Somalia. The pirates took it, and the owners paid the ransom. That's how we know there will be ecstasy on board. We assume that it will be unloaded after dark and then transported to the warehouse. We'll wait for the shipment and then move in."

Kane pointed at the picture. "What's this here?"

Thurston frowned. "It's an SUV."

"What's it doing there? Is it the DEA?"

"No, the DEA are in a building out of shot."

"Have you got other pictures?" Kane asked.

The general showed them to him one at a time, and the

same SUV was in every shot. Kane checked out the time and date stamps. All had been taken at different times over the past few days. He said, tapping his finger on the vehicle in the photo, "Someone else is watching the warehouse, and we need to find out who."

———

Wilmington, *North Carolina*

Set up in a large warehouse two minutes' drive from their target building, the team gathered around a table for their briefing. The warehouse, previously used to store furniture and other imported products, now played host to mice, rats and Team Reaper. Spread out on the battered tabletop was everything they had by way of pictures and intel.

Kane stared at Cara. "You worked out a plan?"

She took a deep breath and said, "We'll go in with two teams. Carlos and I will go in the front and Brick and Pete, the rear."

Kane glanced at Traynor. It made sense to use the ex-DEA man since they were a member down.

"Axe will be here," she said, stabbing a finger at one of the photos. "There's a shipping container over here which will make a good sniper nest for him. He's not too close but in saying that, not too far away either. Once we cross the perimeter, we'll take out the guards, and both teams will breach simultaneously. From there we'll clear the building and secure it. Hopefully, we'll find our HVT. Once that's done, the DEA can come in and take over."

"Sounds simple enough, except that we might have another issue."

"What's that, Ma'am?" Brick asked.

Kane said, "When we were looking over the pictures from the UAV, we noticed an SUV which had been staked out over several days. We can only assume that they, too, were watching the target. When we had the DEA check it out, it was gone and hasn't been back."

"So, be aware, people," Thurston said, "and be prepared. Once that shipment arrives, then you're good to go. Cara will have final call whether the team breaches or not. Understood?"

They all nodded.

Swift said, "Once you give me the word, Ma'am, I'll kill the lights."

"The drone overhead will give us all the coverage we need," Reynolds said. "Teller will make sure that no one sneaks up on you."

Thurston glanced at her watch. "All right. We have two hours until we deploy. Check your equipment and get some rest."

———

"Reaper Four in position," Axe said as he settled in behind the M110A1 with the night scope on top. The cold steel of the container surface was hard, but he had been in more uncomfortable positions over the years.

"Reaper Two and Three in position."

"Reaper Five and Bravo Two in position."

"Copy that," said Kane as he watched the big screen before him. "All callsigns in position and ready to go. Now we have to wait for the drugs to show."

"Hey, Reaper?" Axe asked.

"Yeah?"

"How does it feel to be all tucked up in bed, watching this go down?"

"Loving every minute of it, Reaper Four."

"Liar."

Kane glanced at Thurston who stood beside him, headphones on. She could hear everything they said but remained quiet. It was Kane's job to communicate with the team. Her intervention would come only if it were important, or she had appropriate intel to add.

The comms crackled to life. "DEA in position and holding."

"Copy."

The agent in charge was a man named Potts. He seemed OK, and Traynor knew him from another life. The agents he had with him seemed quite capable too. As an afterthought, Kane said, "Any sign of that SUV?"

"Negative."

"We've got movement on the approaches," Axe said from his position. "Looks like an eighteen-wheeler."

"Copy," Kane acknowledged. "Is there any word from your guys at the port, Potts?"

"Negative. Their comms are down. I suspect they're in a blackspot. Around here is a bitch for them."

"See if you can raise them by cell."

"Will do."

Thurston asked in a low voice, "What are you thinking?"

Kane answered without taking his eyes from the screen. "I'm not sure. I don't like it. The fact that we couldn't find the SUV, the DEA team haven't reported the shipment, and now they can't be raised."

"Reaper from Potts. Over."

"Copy."

"I couldn't raise them."

"Send a man over to check them out, Potts. Something isn't right."

"That's what I was thinking. Out."

"Reaper Two, copy?"

"Copy."

"Something isn't right, Cara. Keep your team on their toes."

"Roger."

Kane watched the large screen as the truck approached. In the background, he could hear Cara coordinating her team. *Her team.* It felt strange thinking that way. The eighteen-wheeler swung through the gates in the high, chain-link fence and was met by three guards when it came to a stop. One of the guards walked across to the driver's door while the other two walked to the back of the rig. They halted there, and one of them opened the rear doors.

Muzzle flashes lit up the dark as all hell broke loose when gunfire from inside the container ripped both guards apart.

"Shit!" Kane exclaimed. "They're going to rip off the drugs. Cara! It's a hit."

———

Wilmington
   The Warehouse

When Kane's call came over the comms, Cara's brain kicked into overdrive. She'd already been on edge, but the warning seemed to take every trace of nervousness away, and she was now cool and calm.

"Axe, sitrep?"

"Looks like someone is trying to rip off whatever they have in the warehouse, as well as the truckload of drugs."

"Roger. Brick? Talk to me."

"We're all clear around the back, Reaper Two. The guards have been drawn away by the shooting."

"Reaper Two, we have more incoming," Axe said, breaking in on the transmission. "Looks like three SUVs."

"Damn it."

"There's more getting out of the back of the truck."

"Damn it," Cara cursed. "Reaper One, are you getting this?"

"Roger, Reaper Two. We're looking at ten tangos who've just arrived. I think they might be with those who just climbed from the truck. They appear to be taking out whatever guards were there. You need to stand down and wait."

"What about our HVT? If we miss him, then we don't have anything on the operation. We need to get in there and roll him up."

"It's too dangerous, Cara."

"This is my call, Reaper!"

He paused. "OK. Execute."

Cara's expression turned grim as she started barking orders into her comms. "Slick, kill the power. Axe, clear us a path in there, and Brick, move in. Reaper Team moving."

The lights went out with the power, but the shooting didn't let up. Cara dropped her NVGs over her eyes, and the scene before her turned green. In her ear, she heard Axe say, "Front gate is clear. Shifting target."

"Copy. Moving to front gate."

Behind Cara, Arenas said, "Nothing like a midnight party."

"Are you trying to be funny?"

"Did it work?"

"No."

"I must try harder then."

Brick's voice came over the comms. "Back gate secure. Moving to rear door."

"Copy, Reaper Five."

Cara and Arenas reached the front gate; her suppressed 416 at her shoulder as she swept for targets as its laser sight reaching out like a thin needle through the green haze of the NVGs. She stepped over the first body just inside the entrance and kept moving. Ahead of her, there were more on the ground. Whether they'd been killed by Axe or another source, she couldn't tell, but at least they were no longer a threat.

An armed man stepped around the back of the truck. He was shooting at someone out of sight, the AK in his hands rattling of a hailstorm of lead.

Cara fired two shots, and the man jerked and fell to the pavement. Behind her, she heard Arenas' weapon cough three times as he put another shooter down.

They reached the truck and paused. The gunfire could still be heard, but it was louder, echoing.

"Reaper Four, sitrep?"

"They've moved inside. All of the threats outside have been neutralized."

Cara frowned. Why would they go inside the warehouse? It was darker in there than outside.

Kane came over the comms. "Cara, don't breach. They'll be spraying lead in there for effect. They can't see shit."

Cara said into her mic, "Reaper Five, where are you?"

"In the warehouse. Reaper is right. We'll extract before we pick up a stray bullet."

"No," Cara snapped. "Stay put. Look for the HVT."

"Copy. Continuing mission."

Suddenly, Thurston's voice came over the comms. "Cara, what are you doing?"

"My job, Ma'am. Out."

Cara stepped around the rear of the trailer and moved quickly towards the door of the warehouse. She swung it open and stepped into hell.

CHAPTER 4

Wilmington
The Warehouse

A round screeched past Cara's ear as it ricocheted off the doorjamb, causing her to duck reflexively. "Fuck!" she hissed and stepped forward. She swept the 416 around and fired at the shooter who was spraying bullets wildly, as though they would act like a forcefield from a science fiction movie.

The man's head snapped back, and he dropped into an untidy heap, the AK in his hands clattering to the concrete. She asked into her mic, "Bravo Four, where's the office in this place?"

A pause then Swift said, "Back left corner."

"Copy," Cara acknowledged. "Brick, clear the building. We're going after the HVT."

"Copy that."

"Carlos, are you OK?"

"Ready to move."

"Let's go. We'll clear the building."

They crossed the open space before them on the diagonal towards the back of the building where the office was meant to be. Off to their right, the gunfire seemed to have diminished somewhat, and Cara figured that Brick was almost done clearing the rest of the warehouse.

Before her in the green haze, steel stairs lifted from the warehouse floor and up to the office which was on a mezzanine level with another room below it. On the stairs was a guard wearing ... "Shit, look out!" Cara shouted.

The man on the stairs was sweeping his weapon around in their direction with his NVGs illuminating them just fine. Cara and Arenas hastily dived to the floor, while above them 7.62 rounds sliced through the air that they had just occupied.

Cara rolled to the left and came up on her knees. The 416 fired three times, and the shooter toppled forward, crashing down the steps toward the concrete floor. "The bastards have NVGs," she hissed. "Tell Brick."

"Yes, Ma'am," said Arenas. He pressed the talk button on his mic. "Reaper Five, be aware that some of them have night vision, over."

"Copy."

Stepping over the body, Cara started up the steps. Arenas fell in behind her, watching her six, and when she'd made it halfway, she realized that the shooting had stopped. An eerie silence fell over the interior of the warehouse.

Cara took another step forward up the stairs and paused. She studied the doorway ahead and said into her mic, "Reaper Five, copy?"

"Roger. All clear here, Ma'am." His voice sounded almost deafening now that the noise had died away.

"Copy. Regroup on me."

"Yes, Ma'am."

Cara started forward again; her boots silent on the steel treads. On reaching the doorway, she peered around the opening. The office appeared to be clear. She took one pace inside, and gunfire erupted as a man stepped from behind a wall partition. Bullets hammered around the doorway, chewing out splinters of wood. Cara fired, and the man jerked his weapon upward. His finger was still depressing the trigger, and the gun stitched a line of bullet holes along the ceiling as he fell backward.

By the time he hit the floor, the shooting had stopped, along with his heart. Cara surged forward; Arenas close behind her. The dead shooter was the only one inside, which didn't bode well. She said, "Bravo Four? Reaper Two, copy?"

"Copy, Reaper Two."

"Turn the power back on."

Cara lifted her NVGs, and after a few heartbeats, the lights flickered, illuminating the room. She looked down at the man at her feet and cursed, "Damn it."

Kane's voice came over the comms. "Sitrep, Reaper Two?"

Rolling her eyes in frustration, she said, "We found the HVT, Reaper. Unfortunately, he won't be able to tell us anything."

"Repeat, Reaper Two."

"Dries Janssen is dead. I shot him."

———

Potts looked down at the dead man and shook his head. "Shame you had to kill him. He could have told us a lot of things about the business he and his brother are running."

"Wasn't much I could do at the time," Cara said abruptly, immediately defending her actions.

"I'm not judging. I probably would have killed him myself. I'm just saying it's a shame."

She studied the middle-aged agent-in-charge and said, "You should be able to gather intel and other stuff from the office."

He nodded. "Should be."

An agent approached them from the doorway. "Sir, we found some things you might want to see. You too, Ma'am."

They followed the agent down the stairs and across the floor, past several empty racks until they reached a stack of forty-four-gallon drums. Three were missing their lids. The agent said, "The drums are filled with pills. We only opened three, but we have to assume the rest are the same."

Cara looked at the stacked drums and did a quick mental calculation. "Christ."

"Yes, Ma'am," the agent agreed. "Also, we think we've identified the guys who tried to steal the drugs."

Potts stared at his man. "Who?"

"I'll show you."

They walked across to one of the dead shooters, and the agent pointed at a small tattoo on the side of his neck. "See there?"

"Albanian?"

"Yes, sir."

"Damn it. I wondered how long before they would take to branch out. I guess now we know."

"I thought these guys had been in the States for a while?" Cara asked.

"They have. Just not down this way. Crazy sons of bitches."

"At least we got something," Cara said. "Is there much other intel?"

"What is relevant we'll pass on to Interpol. Maybe they can sweep up his brother. One thing is for sure, he's going to be pissed about the loss of this merchandise on top of the death of his brother."

———

Antwerp, ***Belgium***
   Three Days Later

"Where is his body now?" Dorian Janssen asked Sander.

"The Americans have it."

The hot rage of finding out about his brother's death was gone, replaced by the calculated scheming for which the older Janssen was known.

"I want you to get it back."

Sander studied his boss before nodding. "It can be done."

"There is more."

"I thought there might be."

When Janssen was finished giving Sander his instructions, the enforcer knew that he would be lucky to ever see Belgium again. Or those going with him for that matter. But when Janssen asked him whether he could do the job, he nodded dutifully and said once again, "Yes, sir."

———

New York City

One Week Later

Pavli Cano stepped out onto the sidewalk in front of the building where his lavish Lower Manhattan apartment was situated and waited for his driver to show. Beside the Albanian was his lieutenant, Halil Lazani. Both were well-known in the Albanian organized crime world. Probably because Cano was head of it all.

The most-feared criminal in all of New York, Cano and his Albanians outstripped even the most violent street gangs. The few who had stood up to them, when they'd moved in, found out the hard way, and none had done so again. Eventually, they learned that the best thing to do was coexist.

However, of late, that wasn't sufficient for Cano, and they were branching out into other regions, including the Wilmington area. It was just a shame that his team had been killed by the damned people of the Worldwide Drug Initiative. But, so had Dries Janssen, which gave even the darkest cloud a little silver lining.

Cano felt pressure on his back, and a voice said, "Just stand still and climb into the van when it stops."

The Albanian glanced sideways at his lieutenant and noticed him standing stiffly, unmoving. Then he saw the man standing behind him and knew there were two of them. He hissed through clenched teeth, "You will not get away with this, whoever you are. You will be found and killed, so too your family."

"I have no family," the man said.

Cano licked his lips. Something about the situation made him nervous. "Who are you?"

No answer.

Suddenly a dark blue van roared out of the morning traffic, and the rear-sliding door opened. The Albanian was shoved roughly towards the opening. Beside him, he heard a suppressed handgun fire, and Lazani dropped to the sidewalk.

Cano whirled, his eyes blazing, "You fucking –"

His words were cut short when the butt of a suppressed FN-Five Seven hit him between the eyes. Stunned, he staggered groggily, and the men bundled him into the van. The door slammed shut, and the vehicle roared away from the curb, leaving the body of Cano's dead lieutenant in a pool of blood on the sidewalk.

———

El Paso, Texas
   Two Days Later

Cara's running route always took her close to the border. She didn't know why, but it was just the way she chose to run. She would leave her place of residence just after daylight and then run for an hour to an hour and a half, depending on how she felt.

This morning, however, her run was interrupted by the ring-tone of her cell. She reached into her fanny pack and took it out. Cara hit answer and held it up to her ear. "Billings."

"Cara, it's Reaper. You have to get back here. There's shit going down over the border, and we've had a call to help out."

"What kind of shit?" she asked. As if on cue, the wind changed, bringing with it the cacophony of gunfire from across the border. "Don't worry, I can hear it. I'm on my way."

Cara hung up and turned to retrace her steps. Coming along the street towards her was a dark van. She glanced at it and then started to run back to HQ.

———

Team Reaper HQ
El Paso, Texas

Kane shoved the last of the freshly-loaded magazines into his webbing and double-checked that he had all he would require for the cross-border op. The call had come in thirty minutes ago. An almost overwhelming force of Juárez Cartel soldiers had a group of *Federales* pinned down in a local no-go zone, and it looked like they were about to be wiped out to a man. When the Mexicans tried to send more of their men in, they'd refused to go. That was when Team Reaper was asked to assist.

Kane, dressed in full combat gear, picked up his 416 and left the lockup. He hurried towards the operations room where he found the team waiting, watching events unfold on the big screen. "How's it looking?"

Thurston walked over to him and said, "From what we can see, most of them are dead. There are maybe four still alive and fighting. They're totally surrounded."

"Why the hell did they go in there?"

"They were after an HVT responsible for killing one of their officers. I guess it was a pride thing."

"Have you seen Cara yet?"

"She's not back?"

"No."

Thurston tried to mask her concern before Kane saw it but failed. "I don't like it either. She should be back by now. She was only ten minutes out. Ping her cell."

"Slick," Thurston called across to her computer tech, "ping Cara's cell."

"Yes, Ma'am."

After a few moments, he turned and said, "I found her."

"Bring it up."

A small square appeared within the big screen. It was a map, and the little red dot, which indicated Cara's cell, flashed brightly.

"It's not moving," Kane said.

"No."

Kane turned to Thurston. "Ma'am ..."

"I'll get Pete to take a look. You get your team moving."

"Yes, Ma'am."

———

Ciudad Juárez
Mexico

Since there were only four of them, Team Reaper only took one armored, black SUV across the border. They'd just hit Mexican soil when they received the call from Thurston saying that the last three *Federales* had capitulated and surrendered to the cartel soldiers.

When Kane asked for confirmation whether to continue the mission, Thurston said, "The call is yours to make, Reaper One."

"Copy that, Ma'am. Wait one."

From behind the wheel, Arenas said, "The cartel will hang their headless bodies upside down for the world to see, as a warning for them not to send anyone else into their territory."

"Do you think we can get to them before they do that?"

In answer to the question, the Mexican put his foot down harder on the gas. He asked Axe and Brick, "You fellers good with this?"

"I'm all for saving lives," said the ex-SEAL.

"Axe?"

"I'm bored sitting around all the time. Let's do it."

Kane nodded. "Reaper One to Bravo."

"Copy, Reaper."

"We're going in. Have Slick keep us updated. Any word on UAV clearance?"

"Negative on the UAV."

"Copy."

"Good luck."

"Ma'am. Reaper One out."

The SUV bumped along the streets as Arenas kept it at a steady clip. He reached an intersection and turned left off the main thoroughfare into a narrower side street. He sped up again, and Kane pressed his comms button. "We're about two minutes out. Sitrep."

Swift came over the radio and said, "Reaper One. It looks like they're getting ready to execute the prisoners."

"Copy."

Arenas took the next turn at speed, and the rear of the SUV fishtailed before whipping back into line on the empty street. On their left, another street rose up and turned into an overpass. From the backseat, Axe snapped, "Stop here!"

"What?" Kane asked.

"Stop the hell here."

The Mexican slammed on the brakes, and the vehicle shuddered to a stop. The rear door flew open, and Axe leaped out with his M110A1 sniper system. Kane rolled down his side window and shouted after the ex-recon man. "Where are you going?"

"Up!"

Kane saw the six-story building he was running towards and nodded. He said to Arenas, "Go. He'll be fine."

The SUV shot forward once more, and the last Kane saw of his man was when he looked in the side mirror and caught him disappearing into the lobby of the building.

Brick said, "What are we going to do once we arrive?"

Kane turned his head and smiled, instantly causing the ex-SEAL to regret opening his mouth. "We're going to improvise."

"And if that don't work?"

"We'll shoot them and go home."

"Sounds like a plan."

Suddenly they were there. The buildings on their left stopped, and everything opened out, revealing the overpass and a mess of bodies dressed in dark blue with black tactical gear. An SUV was burning off to one side, while armed men covered in tattoos, carrying AK-47s, stood not far away looking up at a man dangling upside down from the overpass. His clothes had been removed, and he was hanging low enough for those below to reach him. Against the background of aged concrete and graffiti, the man looked unnaturally pale.

The vehicle skidded to a halt, and Kane said, "Lock and load. If you have to shoot, shoot to kill."

They came out of the SUV, 416s raised and aimed at the immediate threats. Three men, all heavily-tattooed and armed with AKs started to approach them, seemingly unbothered by the new intruders. Probably because there were another twenty or so armed men behind them. What threat could three more be?

One of them stepped further forward than the others. He had a tattooed face and a gold-toothed smile. Kane figured him to be a shot-caller.

"I see we have *Gringo* heroes come over the border to interfere with cartel business," he said in an assured manner. "Maybe if you get back in your car, we will let you go for this minor indiscretion. Yes?"

"Reaper Four in position," Axe said in Kane's ear. "Just say when."

"Who are you?" Kane asked the cartel man.

"I am Marcius Montero. But mostly, people call me *La Serpiente*." His tongue flickered out, revealing the crude split in the end of it.

Kane knew of the *Sicario* for the Juárez Cartel. Mean and bloody was what he'd heard. Well-known for the exact thing that he was about to do to his prisoners.

"What if we don't?" Kane asked him.

Montero raised his left hand to shoulder height, and one of the cartel soldiers next to the hanging *Federale* stepped in close to him and cut his throat.

The dying man jerked violently before his struggles faded and then ceased.

"Motherfucker," Axe hissed. "Let me put a bullet in this prick's head."

Behind him, Kane sensed Brick move further to his right so the ex-SEAL could clear his line of fire. Arenas on the left didn't have to; his had been clear since they'd left the SUV.

"Reaper One, cleared to engage," Ferrero said into his ear.

Kane took one last look around the area, mentally recording the positions of each cartel soldier.

Again, Ferrero's voice came to him. "Do it now, Reaper. Slick just picked up a transmission calling for more men. They're not going to let you out of there."

Then Kane's gaze drifted back to the smiling man. He said to Montero, "You ever heard the expression that out there somewhere there's a bullet with your name on it?"

El Paso, Texas

Traynor pulled the Tahoe over to the curb and stared at the sight before him. Police cruisers, crime-scene tape, a medical examiner's van, and reporters. "This isn't good," he said to himself.

The ex-DEA agent climbed from the vehicle and approached the crowd. He pushed his way through until he made it to the tape where a uniformed officer was standing. He reached inside his pocket and took out his ID. Traynor held it up and asked, "What's going on?"

"Who are you?" the officer asked.

"Traynor. Worldwide Drug Initiative."

"Never heard of it."

"We fight bad guys."

"Nope."

"Can you tell me what happened?"

"Nope."

"Can I speak to someone in charge?"

The cop shook his head. "They're all busy."

Traynor sighed with frustration. "Look, I'm looking for

a friend whose cell phone says they're over there. I need information."

"Can't help you."

There was a violent scuffle further along the tape between two reporters, dragging the officer's attention away as he walked towards the brawling pair. With the officer's back turned, Traynor slipped under the obstruction and hurried towards the crime scene.

"Hey! Who the hell are you?" a man called out. Traynor turned and stared at him. Detective.

"Stop right there," the man growled and started forward. Traynor reached into his pocket again and retrieved his ID.

The detective was solidly-built and looked angry at the intrusion. He stopped short and stared at Traynor's credentials. "Who the hell is that?"

"We fight bad guys," Traynor said to him.

"Well, you can fight them over the other side of the tape. Get out of here."

"I need to know if the body you have is one of ours."

"How do you know we have a body?"

"I'm not dumb. I worked DEA before the job I have now. There is a cell phone pinging here somewhere, and it belongs to one of our own. It's a woman."

The detective asked, "What's your name?"

"Pete Traynor. Like it says on my ID."

"I'm Wallis. This is my crime scene. And to put your mind at rest, the stiff isn't a woman."

"Did you find a cell?"

The detective nodded. He reached into his pocket and took out an evidence bag. "This it?"

Traynor took it and said, "Yeah, that's it. What happened?"

"We're not real sure. There were no witnesses, and all we have is the body of a Caucasian male who's taken two rounds to the chest."

"Is that it?"

"That's about it. So, if that cell belongs to your friend, then it doesn't look good for her."

"You're right about that. Do you mind if I get a picture of the dead guy?"

The detective nodded. "Sure."

They walked over to where the corpse lay. Wallis pulled back the cover sheet, and Traynor took a picture with his cell. The dead man had brown hair, and two bullet wounds right where the detective said they were. Traynor put his cell away and said, "I'm done."

"Listen," Wallis said, "leave me your number, and if something else turns up, I'll call."

"That'd be great, thanks."

CHAPTER 5

Ciudad Juárez
Mexico

The *sicario* frowned. "What the fuck you on about, *puta?*"

The 7.62 round whistled out of the emptiness and hit with the wet sound of an egg being dropped on the pavement. Montero's eyes flew wide as his brains exploded out the side of his head and splattered on the ground beside him. A shout erupted from one of the Mexicans with him as he fought to bring his AK up to fire.

Kane's 416 beat him to it, and rounds from a short burst punched into the cartel soldier's chest. The dying man fell to the ground, and the Team Reaper leader shifted aim to focus on the second Mexican.

The 416s of Arenas and Brick opened up and spat lead death at the stunned cartel soldiers. Their firing was the methodical rhythm of well-trained operators used to being shot at. Not the panicked spraying which these shooters were accustomed to.

The second cartel man that Kane fired at died when a 5.56mm slug crashed through half-rotted teeth and deflected up into his brain.

Kane shouted above the gunfire at the two remaining *Federales*, "Get down! Get down!"

Whether or not they understood English didn't matter for they seemed to understand what he wanted them to do, and they dropped to the rough ground.

The 416 in Brick's hands fired twice, shifted aim, and fired twice more. A large cartel soldier well in excess of six-feet lurched back with two rounds in his barrel chest and two in his throat.

Meanwhile, Axe kept sending in 7.62 missiles with brutal efficiency, the image of the naked *Federale* with his throat slashed burned deep into his brain. He saw one of the tattooed killers go to hose down the prisoners with a Micro-Uzi, but before he could, the ex-recon marine put a bullet in his head.

Bullets kicked up grit around Arenas' feet as a cartel man cranked out a full magazine from his AK. Showing no sign of fear, the former Mexican special forces commander brought a halt to the wild fusillade.

"Push forward!" Kane shouted as he slapped home a fresh magazine into the 416. "Push forward!"

The other two men moved with him as he started taking steps towards the prisoners as they tried to secure them.

"Changing!" Brick called out as his magazine ran dry. Kane stopped moving while the ex-SEAL changed out the empty magazine and replaced it with a fully-loaded one. Suddenly he grunted and dropped to the ground.

"Brick!" Kane shouted and hurried to his comrade, ignoring the swarm of angry leaden hornets buzzing around his head.

He crouched over the fallen man and checked for blood. There was none; the round had impacted the ex-SEAL's armor. As he removed the vest and webbing, he said into his comms, "This is Reaper One. Reaper Five is down. I say again, Reaper Five is down."

"What's his status, Reaper One?" Ferrero asked, his voice unwavering.

"He seems to be OK. His armor took the impact. He's just –"

Brick gasped as he sucked great gulps of air into his lungs. He coughed and tried to sit up. "Stay there," Kane said. "We've got this."

Brick moaned and did as ordered. Kane lurched back to his feet and brought his 416 up, relieved that his man was fine. "Zero? Reaper One. Reaper Five is OK. Continuing mission."

"Copy, Reaper One."

As he swept the scene before him searching for a target, Kane suddenly realized that there were no more cartel soldiers left. "Axe, sitrep?"

"Looks clear from here, Reaper."

"Roger. Carlos, let's get these *Federales* into the SUV and get the hell out of here."

"Copy, Reaper."

He hurried forward to where the two men were cowering on the ground. Reaching down, he touched one of them. "Get up. It is over. Hurry."

One of the men looked up at Reaper, his face bloody and etched deep with fear. Arenas guessed his law enforcement days were done. He said to the man, "It is OK, Amigo. Help your friend to his feet. We need to leave before more of them come."

The man nodded jerkily and started to climb to his feet.

He helped his friend up, and they stood there shaking. Arenas pressed his talk button. "Reaper, these guys are in shock. They need medical attention."

"Roger that. Get them in the back of the SUV and use the blankets from the cargo bay. Take them over to El Paso and get them to a medical center. Take Brick with you. We need to get him checked out."

"What about you and Axe?"

"We'll –" Kane stopped mid-sentence.

Arenas looked across at him and saw his commander staring away to his right. Approaching them from across the small killing field was a young woman with long dark hair. She stopped to check each corpse as she went. Through his comms, Arenas heard Kane mutter, "What the hell?"

"What is this, Amigo?"

"I'm not sure. Get those men into the SUV and wait for my word."

Arenas gathered the two survivors while his commander walked over to the woman. As he did so, he said to Axe, "Keep an eye out. We'll have tangos inbound shortly."

"Roger."

The young woman stood up from checking one of the cartel soldiers and seemed surprised to see Kane standing before her. She stepped backward and tensed as though she was about to run when Kane said, "Whoa, I'm not going to hurt you. We're friendly. We were sent to help the police."

Recognition flickered across her face. "You are American?"

"Yes. My name is Kane. Who are you?"

She stepped around him and hurried across to the next body. "I'm Doctor Rosanna Morales."

"A doctor? What are you doing here?"

She stood erect and stared coldly at him. She indicated the bodies and said, her voice filled with sarcasm, "I don't know. What do you think?"

Kane winced at the venom in her voice. "It's a waste of time checking them. They're all dead."

"How do you know?"

"There wasn't time to do anything else. Listen, you shouldn't be here, you need to leave. There are more of them coming."

Ignoring him, she continued her preoccupation with checking the next corpse. Kane cursed under his breath and said, "We have two *Federales* in our SUV. Both are in shock. Plus, I have a man who took a round to his chest plate." He indicated Brick, who stood hunched over, still feeling the effects of the bullet. "He needs to be looked at too."

"Reaper One? Bravo Four. Suggest you get out of there. Two vehicles inbound your position, over."

"Copy, Bravo Four," Kane answered. "Ma'am, we need to get out of here."

"Why?"

"Because there are more cartel people coming, and if they find you here, they will take their anger out on you."

"I had nothing to do with this."

He stared into her brown eyes to get his point across. "They aren't much going to care. Like I said, we have people you can help."

Rosanna nodded. "OK, I will come with you. But only to help the men who require it."

"Good. Thank you," Kane said to her and then pressed his talk button. "Axe, wind it up. We'll get you on the way out."

"Roger. I'm moving now."

"Zero? Reaper One. Copy?"

"Copy, Reaper One."

"Were extracting now. We'll be bringing plus three."

"Copy, Reaper."

"Reaper One, out."

By the time they were all loaded into the SUV, Brick was finally coming around. One thing was for sure; he would have a right pretty bruise at the end of the day. When they pulled away from the slaughter zone, the doctor was in the back of the SUV, checking on the *Federales*. Kane turned and called over his shoulder, "How are they doing?"

"You were right. They're in shock and need a hospital."

"Will they be right until we get them across the border?"

Rosanna looked surprised. "No one will see them over the border."

"We'll take them to William Beaumont Army Medical Center."

"It will still be the same."

"It's OK, we know someone."

The SUV came to a halt, and the back door on the passenger side opened. Axe leaped in and glanced over the back seat, taking in the passengers. He smiled at Rosanna and said, "Well, hello there, *Senorita*."

"It's Doctor."

"I stand corrected," he grinned and turned and stared at Brick. "How you feeling, buddy?"

"Like I forgot to duck," he groaned as the vehicle hit a bump.

"I got shot once. Hurt like a bitch. Actually, make that twice. Or was it three times? I –"

"Axe?"

"Yeah?"

"Shut up."

"Yeah."

By the time they reached William Beaumont Army Medical Center, the nurses and doctors there were expecting them. Kane had called Thurston who went up the chain to General Hank Jones, the Chairman of the Joint Chiefs.

They left Brick there with the *Federales* under protest. Kane assured him that there would be a beer waiting for him when he got out. "There better be."

When the team left, they took Rosanna with them back to their HQ to be debriefed by Thurston. No sooner had they pulled up when Traynor came out to meet them, a grim expression on his face. "What's up?" Kane asked him.

He paused for a moment and then said, "Cara's missing."

———

Outside El Paso

Cara kicked and thrashed as they dragged her hooded form from the back of the van. She felt her foot catch one of her abductors and heard him curse. A fist crashed into her stomach, and the air whooshed from her lungs, exploding around the foul gag in her mouth.

Cara's body went limp, and the men either side of her almost dropped her to the ground. Boots crunched on gravel and more voices reached her ears. Cara listened. What were they? European? She needed to get the hood off somehow to see. She'd had it on since being taken off the street soon after she'd hung up from the call to Reaper.

After the initial flurry of violence, her resistance, them punching, Cara had lost track of her position and what direction they had traveled. One thing she was sure of, they weren't in Mexico.

Before she knew what was happening, the hood was torn roughly from her head, revealing a bruised left cheek and a thin line of dried blood emanating from the corner of her mouth beneath the gag. She had sustained the injuries while being abducted from the street after she'd shot the man they had left behind.

Blinking to allow her eyes to adjust to the sun's glare, Cara growled like a caged animal. A large man with a black beard came into view. He reached out with his right hand and wrapped strong fingers around the struggling woman's throat. The intense pressure ceased her movements immediately.

"You have already killed one of my men today. If you keep this up, I will snap your neck like a twig. Understand?"

Cara nodded.

"Good. Get her on the plane."

The men on either side of her started to push her clumsily towards a Gulfstream G600. Cara glanced about, attempting to make out any familiar landmark which might indicate where she was. Somewhere outside of El Paso at an old airfield. But there were plenty of those.

They forced her up the steps and in through the door, then through the cabin until she reached a three-seat lounge towards the back of the plane. One of the seats was occupied by a man. Cara glanced at him, noticing that although he was expensively dressed, his face bore similar markings to hers.

The big man with the beard came to the rear of the plane and removed Cara's gag. She stared at him and asked, "Where are you taking me?"

His gaze lingered upon her as though he was considering telling her. Then, "You will find that out when we arrive."

"Fucking asshole," the man in the opposite seat hissed in accented English.

The bearded man's left hand flashed out and crashed against the prisoner's cheek, silencing him.

"Who are you?" Cara asked him, changing tack.

"I am Sander."

"Can't you at least tell me where you are taking me?"

The airtight door at the front of the plane was closed and latched. Sander smiled and said, "Buckle up; we are about to take off."

He turned away from her and crossed to another sofa on the other side of the plane and sat, buckling himself in, waiting for the plane to start moving.

The two Pratt and Whitney turbofan engines came to life with a whine, each capable of hurling the jet along the runway with approximately fifteen and a half thousand pounds of thrust. After a few minutes, the plane began to move and taxied towards the single runway. At six thousand feet, the runway came in just over the required distance for the jet to be able to take off.

Looking out the small window, Cara saw the dry landscape slide by, and in the distance, there was a rundown building with a control tower attached to the top of it. She frowned. Golden Field. It had to be. It had been named after Chuck Golden, a World War Two vet who'd been awarded the Congressional Medal after Peleliu. It had been shut down some ten years before, but obviously, the runway was still usable.

The Gulfstream reached the end of the tarmac and turned. It remained stationary while the pilot pushed the throttles forward all the way. The engines climbed to a screech, and then the brakes were released. Cara felt herself being forced back in her seat as the plane picked up speed. The nose of the Gulfstream rose, followed by the rear wheels as they left the ground.

———

Team Reaper HQ
El Paso

The first breakthrough came an hour after the team arrived back from across the border. Swift had been doing all he could to narrow down what had happened. Then he got a hit on the picture of the dead guy that Traynor had taken.

The dead guy's name was Evert Alting. He was a Belgian national who at one stage in his life had been Belgian SFG. Next, Swift tried to see if the name came up on any flight manifests over the past month but drew a blank. However, his search through Interpol came back interesting. It seemed that Interpol had him marked as being a low-level employee of one Dorian Janssen.

Then for the next hour, Swift used his skills to find others who flew under the Janssen banner and ran them through facial recognition amongst the many security cameras around El Paso.

He came up with two more. A big man named Sander and another called Filip Claasen. Both men were also former Belgian SFG. Swift did another search trying to match faces with aliases, but still, nothing popped. He widened the search and came up with Sander and Alting in New York. Still with nothing indicating how they'd got into the country, but there was something else interesting. About the same time that they were there, Pavli Cano, the Albanian Organized Crime boss disappeared and his hitter, Lazani was killed on the street outside of his apartment building. Witnesses said that he was last seen being forced into a van after Lazani had been shot on the sidewalk.

Slowly a picture was starting to form, and Swift didn't like it.

He knew that they had to have come in somewhere, so he searched Janssen and came up with a privately-owned Gulfstream. A few more searches and it all came together. Time to talk to the boss.

He found Thurston in her office, talking to Kane and Rosanna. Looking up at Swift, she said, "What is it?"

"I've got something you'll all want to see."

"Cara?" Kane asked.

"It could be. It's a theory."

Thurston nodded. "OK. We'll meet in the briefing room. I'll get everyone together in five minutes."

"Yes, Ma'am."

Swift left, and Thurston turned her gaze to Rosanna. "As you see, there is never a dull moment. Will you at least consider my offer?"

Rosanna nodded. "I will think about it. But I am a Mexican citizen. If I was to come and work for you, how would we get past that?"

Thurston smiled. "I know a man."

The doctor nodded. "I do not shoot guns. I will not even touch one."

"I wouldn't expect you to."

Again, another nod.

"What do you think, Reaper?"

"I think that the addition to the team would be beneficial, Ma'am."

"I agree. Come and sit in on the briefing, Rosanna. You'll get an idea on how we operate."

The doctor glanced sideways at Kane. "I've seen how one part of you operates."

"Now, you can see how the rest of us do it."

———

Team Reaper HQ
Briefing Room

Once the team was gathered, Thurston handed the floor over to Swift so he could do his thing. He tapped a key on his laptop computer, revealing a picture of the dead man Traynor had snapped with another beside it of when Alting was still alive.

"Who are we looking at, Slick?" Thurston asked.

"This is Evert Alting. He's former Belgian SFG, but as you can see, he's as dead as a dodo. Thanks, we think, to Cara."

"Can you be sure of that?" Ferrero asked.

"No, sir. It's just a guess."

Ferrero nodded.

Swift continued, "I did the usual searches and came up with these two men. Sander Aakster and Filip Claasen. Both ex-SFG. Aakster is the good-looking guy who resembles Axe."

"You mean; looks like a puckered asshole with fur around it?" Brooke Reynolds asked.

The muffled chuckle in the room was punctuated with an indignant, "That's just cruel, that is. I'm bleeding."

"All right, knock it off," Thurston said. "Continue, Slick."

"All three of these men were picked up on cameras throughout El Paso over the past three days. Previously, they sprang up in New York. This was about the same time as Pavli Cano was taken from the street outside his apartment block, and his enforcer Halil Lazani was shot on the street when it happened."

"Isn't Cano the Albanian organized crime boss?" Traynor asked.

Swift nodded.

Kane leaned forward on his seat. "Are you saying that the abductions of Cano and Cara are connected?"

"It looks that way, although I don't have hard evidence."

"What do you have?"

"I did a search through Interpol, and each one of these guys is known to them. The interesting part was that they all work for Dorian Janssen."

"Shit!" Kane hissed. "This is some kind of revenge bullshit, isn't it? It was Janssen's brother that Cara killed in Wilmington, and it was Cano's crew that attacked the warehouse."

"It looks that way."

"Well, let's get out there and find the bastards," Axe growled.

"That would be a waste of time," Swift told them.

"Why?" Thurston inquired.

"I tried to find something that might point to how they got into the country. At first, I came up with nothing. Then once I broadened my search parameters, I found a Gulf-stream belonging to Janssen. That is how they got into the country."

He hit another key on his computer, and a satellite image appeared showing an airfield. Swift moved closer to the screen and pointed to something white at the center of the screen. "This is it, here. The picture was taken four hours ago."

"Where is that?" Kane asked.

"Golden Field, outside of El Paso."

"Why do I feel there is a big but coming?" Ferrero asked.

The screen changed. "This was taken thirty minutes ago."

The picture was clear, no plane.

"It's gone," Arenas said.

Swift nodded. "Yes."

Kane came to his feet and looked at Thurston. "Ma'am, it seems pretty straight forward to me."

Thurston stared at the picture. "It would seem to be too much of a coincidence."

"We need to get spun up," Kane urged.

"What we need is confirmation," the general told him.

"We can't just sit here and do nothing, Ma'am," Kane said testily. "We did that once, and it cost a man his life."

"Do you have any idea how much it costs to get this team to Europe?" Thurston asked calmly. "If I pull the trigger on this, and believe me I'd rather do nothing else, and she's not there, it's my ass in a sling for making the wrong call. The first thing I'll be asked when I front a Senate inquiry is, why didn't you wait for confirmation?"

"That's bullshit, Ma'am," Kane growled.

"Kane!" Ferrero snapped.

Thurston said, "I agree. But if she has been taken to Belgium by Janssen, it is for a reason. Otherwise, she'd be dead beside the man on the street." Her voice hardened. "Now, stand down. That's an order."

Kane could tell by the look in her eyes that she wasn't going to take any more. Not willing to push her further, he replied, "Yes, Ma'am."

"But just in case, I want everything ready to go. Reaper, you're in charge of the armory. If we get a positive ID, I want everything to run smoothly so we can be wheels up at a moment's notice. I'll have the C-17 on standby. Everyone understand what they have to do?"

They all nodded.

"Traynor, you'll be on standby as part of Reaper Team just in case they need you."

"Yes, Ma'am."

"You OK with that, Reaper?"

"Yes, Ma'am."

"Good, let's get to it. Luis, can I have a word?"

Everyone went about their business while Ferrero and the general moved off to one side. "I'm going to reach out to a few contacts to see what we can find out about Janssen and if there's someone who can find out if Cara is on that damned plane. Keep an eye on Reaper. I don't want a repeat of what happened with Axe."

"I'll do that, Mary. He'll be fine."

CHAPTER 6

Antwerp, Belgium

The flight to Antwerp took ten hours. Ten hours that felt like twice that long, sitting, wondering what was in store for her, and by the time the plane landed at a small airfield, Cara was exhausted physically and mentally. She was escorted from the plane, and once on the tarmac, noticed a black SAAB SUV waiting no further than twenty meters away in the darkness.

As tired as she was, Cara's training had her taking in her surroundings, trying to make out any distinguishing features. "Where are we?" she asked Sander.

"Belgium."

"Why are we here?"

There was a yelp from behind her, and Cara whirled about just in time to see Cano fall down the steps to the tarmac. Groaning, the Albanian was quickly yanked upright by his collar by Claasen who had been behind him on the steps.

When the door of the SAAB opened, the interior light came on, and she noted the driver. A man of average height and build climbed out from the rear door. Cara figured him to be middle-aged. He was dressed in a suit and strode towards the plane with determined purpose.

She watched him walk across to the Albanian and stand in front of him. A few words were spoken, and Cano seemed to pale somewhat. Then Cara watched on in horror as the man drew a sidearm and shot the Albanian in the head.

Cara's head jerked at the crash of the weapon, and then her heart raced as she considered the stark reality that she could be next. The shooter turned and stared in her direction before approaching, weapon still visible down at his side. He stopped just short, his gray eyes burning holes into her, making her swallow involuntarily.

"My name is Dorian Janssen," he said. "You killed my brother."

Then he raised the gun.

―――――

The SAAB came to a halt on the gravel turnaround, and the motor was switched off. Opening the doors, Janssen and his men climbed out. Sander's boots crunched on the gravel as he walked around behind the vehicle. He opened the rear door and reached in, pulling a bound and gagged Cara from the luggage area.

Sander helped her stay erect, and once she'd found her feet, Cara again tried to pick out features in her surroundings. The house was huge. Cara guessed it was all paid for by Janssen's drug empire. It was a classic double story affair with mullioned windows, and she could just make out two stone chimneys. The gardens and surrounds were thick, and she assumed lush. A flower bed beneath one of the windows was illuminated by the light shining through it, the blooms brightly-colored.

"Get her in the house," Janssen snapped. "Put her in the study and guard her. I'll be there shortly."

Sander guided her up the front steps to the solid wood door. He opened it and shoved her through into an opulent foyer. It was brightly lit by a massive chandelier, which looked as though it needed a crane to keep it in place. A grand staircase was in front of her, and at the landing, one had a choice to turn left or right. The enforcer closed the door behind them and steered Cara towards another solid wood door; this one a darker color. Sander opened this one too, and once Cara was inside, he pushed her onto a leather lounge.

Straight away, she noticed the thick plastic on the carpet. Her blood ran cold as she thought of many movies, she'd seen with the stuff on the floor right before someone died.

Nervously, Cara jiggled her legs, waiting for Janssen to join them. Part of her wished he'd just killed her after she had gotten off the plane, instead of torturing her with the wait. He came into the room five minutes later, and she prepared herself for the inevitable. In the light, she could see him better. The graying hair, the lined face. She snapped, "Just kill me and get it over with, asshole."

His smile was cold, almost cruel. He stood there in silence, waiting, wanting to draw the tension out even further. In the end, Janssen said, "I'm not going to kill you. Not like you did my brother. No, I have something more special in store for you."

"Like what?" Cara snapped, more than a little relieved that she would remain alive for the foreseeable future.

"My brother was everything to me. He was all the family that I had in this world. Now he is gone, and you are responsible."

"How do you know I was the one?"

Cara realized that it was a dumb question, even before the words were out of her mouth. In this day and age, anything you needed to know was reasonably easy to find out.

"Do I really need to answer that question?"

"I guess not. So, what will happen now if you're not going to kill me?"

"In a couple of days, I will have a visitor. He is a dealer in the flesh. If he likes you, and we can come to an arrangement, then you will be sold to him. You see, I don't want you dead. You cannot reflect on what you have done if you are this way. I want you to remember it every day—every waking moment. I want you to wish you were dead. When a stinking Belarussian worker is humping your brains out, I want you to know *why*."

At the sight of the crazy look in Janssen's eyes, a cold shiver ran down Cara's spine. The guy was seriously unhinged. Her eyes narrowed. "You're insane," she hissed. "Too much of your own product."

Janssen smiled coldly. "Maybe. I guess one day we'll find out. Take her away and lock her in the room upstairs."

Cara's stomach growled. She knew that if she were to get through this, it would require all her strength. "What about something to eat?"

Her captor stared at her for a moment as he considered his answer. Then he nodded. "Find her something from the kitchen. Is there anything else?"

"I suppose a beer is out of the question?"

Janssen chuckled. "Sure, why not? Sander will take care of it for you."

The enforcer led Cara into a kitchen which was the size of the local café in El Paso where she often ate. Marble countertops, an island the size of two standard ones in the center of the room, two stainless steel refrigerators, more cupboards than she'd ever seen at one time, and exposed copper pipes on the walls which supplied water to twin sinks.

All this would have wowed any guest to the house, but not Cara. Her focus was centered on the knife block on the countertop to her left, next to a stainless-steel coffee maker. She shuffled across just a fraction. Sander opened one of the refrigerators and peered inside.

Cara moved again.

Backing out of the refrigerator with two bottles of Heineken, Sander cracked the top and passed one across to Cara, kicking the door closed with the toe of his boot. She stared at him, curiously. The big man took a sip and placed the bottle on the counter. He then walked across to the other refrigerator and opened it.

With swift movements, Cara moved to the knife block and took one of the smaller ones. She cursed inwardly while she tried to find a place to hide it. Eventually, she tucked it behind her back into her running pants and pulled her top down over it.

Sander stepped away from the refrigerator with an armful of food. He dumped it on the island bench and stabbed at it with a finger. "Eat."

For the next ten minutes, Cara ate and drank her beer while Sander watched on in silence. When she was finished, he escorted her upstairs to a large room with a double bed and bathroom. "You will stay here."

"I could use some clean clothes," Cara told him.

Sander grunted and turned away, walking toward the door. Suddenly he stopped as though he'd forgotten something. He pivoted and held out his hand. Cara frowned. "What?"

He raised his eyebrows and waited.

"Shit," Cara swore and reached back for the knife. She handed it over, and Sander gave her a brief smile. Then without a further word, he turned and left the room, locking the door behind him.

"Double shit."

————

Team Reaper HQ
El Paso

General Mary Thurston disconnected her call and tossed the phone on her desk. She hurried out into the operations area of the team's headquarters where she found Ferrero, Kane, and Swift going over some reports. They looked up at her approach, and by the expression on her face, they knew that after two days she had some news.

"I just got off a call from Interpol. Belgian police found Cano in some woods outside of Antwerp. It was only by luck that a hiker stumbled across it."

"Cara?" Kane asked.

Thurston shook her head. "Nothing. But I'm ready to pull the trigger on this thing. Call everyone together, Luis, I need to phone Hank."

"Yes, Ma'am."

She whirled away and went back to her office, where she picked up the phone and rang Hank Jones.

"Hello, Mary," his voice came down the line. "How're things? You found that MIA of yours yet?"

"Not yet, sir, but we may have a lead."

"Fill me in."

Thurston ran through with him what she'd been told from her call with Interpol. When she finished, Jones said, "And I take it that you want permission to go operational?"

"Yes, sir. I know that it's not convincing, but I feel it in my gut, sir."

"You're right, Mary, it is thin. However, I'm willing to take a chance on your gut. Heaven forbid that we never acted and something untoward happened."

"Thank you, sir."

"Don't thank me yet. You haven't heard the rest of it. Take only those you need. The others will stay home. If they are required, you can fly them out. If you had concrete proof, then I would sign off on sending the lot of you. Are we clear?"

"Yes, sir."

"Well, OK then. Good luck, Mary."

"Thank you, sir."

Jones disconnected, and Thurston left her office and went back to the operations room. She called Kane and Ferrero over and told them of Jones' orders.

"What are you going to do?" Ferrero asked.

"I'll take Reaper's team and Swift and Pete Traynor. You, Teller, and Reynolds can hold down the fort. Are you OK with that?"

Ferrero nodded. "I'm more than good with that. Since I was off sick, I've still not felt one hundred percent."

Thurston nodded. "Should we need UAV support, Brooke and Teller can operate it from here. I'm only taking Traynor because he can alternate in the field or be an extra gun for us at base."

"Where are you going to operate from?" Ferrero asked.

"Interpol in Brussels have a place we can set up. They've said they'll help us all they can. If it means that they'll be rid of Janssen, they're more than happy."

"When are we leaving, Ma'am?" Kane asked.

"Just as soon as we can get that blasted plane in the air."

CHAPTER 7

Antwerp, Belgium

Aleksey Kazan was a bad man. Of Russian and Belarussian breeding, he'd started in the flesh trade the day he resigned from the State Security Agency of the Republic of Belarus, otherwise known as Belarus' KGB. He'd walked out of his office in the afternoon, shot a man for his business in the evening, and taken over his empire with the help of contacts he'd cultivated over the years.

Now, the forty-eight-year-old man, with the hair lip and gray hair, ran a pipeline from the west which carried young women east to countries such as Romania, Bulgaria, and Ukraine; holding auctions once a month to sell the girls he acquired.

The German and French girls were always his best sellers. Every now and then an American or a blonde Swedish girl fetched a premium price. Italian girls were OK, so were the British. The Spanish were too much trouble, so he tried to stay clear of them as much as possible.

Kazan was like an octopus. His tentacles spread throughout Europe. At the end of those tentacles were small groups of men who scoured nightclubs and other places frequented by young women.

They had a constant supply of Rohypnol, used for spiking drinks. Once the tablets had taken effect, the drugged girls would be helped outside, given a needle to sedate them properly, and then they would disappear. By the time they realized what was happening, it was too late. The girls were halfway across Europe.

When Kazan's car pulled up in the turnaround at Janssen's mansion, he had a feeling that this deal was going to be far from ordinary. For starters, the girl was actually a woman in her thirties. An age that he would normally never consider, as his clients wanted young flesh. But he had an upcoming auction which might prove successful in moving her. If not, he would work something out.

Janssen came out to meet him, and the two shook hands. "It is good to see you, Aleksey. I trust your journey was good?"

"It was OK. I was in Germany wrapping up some business when I received your call. I must tell you now that I normally would not even consider making a purchase of a woman of such age. But since you are a friend, I am willing to make an exception."

Nodding, Janssen said, "I appreciate you taking the time. However, I'm not selling this woman. I am offering her to you as a favor to me."

Surprise registered on Kazan's face. "Really?"

"Come inside, and I shall explain it all."

———

Cara stood in her comfortable prison, staring out the window at the two men talking below. Janssen she knew, but the other man she'd never seen before. Although she had the overwhelming feeling that this man was here for her.

Apart from food and drink, she'd been left alone for the past few days. But that was all about to change; she was sure of it. The key turned in the lock to her room. The door swung open, and Sander entered. He stared at the clothes she was wearing. They had been supplied to her the day after she'd arrived in Belgium. Jeans, a white cotton shirt with a singlet beneath it. He said, "You come."

"Just like that. You bark, and I jump?"

"Hmm," Sander grumbled.

"What if I don't want to?"

"Then I will make you."

"Try it?"

Sander closed the gap between them and reached out to grasp her left arm. Cara's right fist came up and crashed into the big man's jaw. The blow turned his head marginally, and the sound of it connecting filled the room.

Sander's reaction was reflexive as his own palm flew around and crashed into Cara's left cheek, making her stagger. The flesh burned, and she hit him again, with more force this time.

The reaction was the same, except a little harder. Tears came to Cara's eyes, and she hit him a third time. As soon as the blow connected, she stepped back and threw her hands up. "You win! You hit too hard."

Sander contemplated hitting her anyway but decided not to. Instead, he stood aside and directed her towards the door. Cara walked forward.

"Ahh, here she is," Janssen said as Cara and Sander entered the study.

Kazan turned to look and nodded in appreciation. "So, this is the woman who killed your brother. She doesn't look so tough to me, Dorian."

"Try me, asshole, and I'll cut your bastard heart out."

Kazan shrugged. "Maybe she is. I think I might have a use for her after all."

"What did you do in America?" the flesh-peddler asked. "What was this unit you were with?"

"They're the ones who will kill you when they find you," Cara hissed.

"I like this one. She's feisty. I tell you what; I will give you one million dollars for her."

"I already told you, I don't want money."

"It is only fair, no?" Kazan said. "For I intend to make a lot of money from her. She is going to be a fighter. Entertainment for the guests at the auctions. What do you think of that, *detka*?"

"Yebat' tebya mudak." Cara hissed.

Kazan laughed out loud. "Maybe, I should make you my wife."

"Maybe, you should fuck off."

He walked slowly over to where Cara stood. He stared into her hate-filled eyes, and suddenly his right hand flashed up and his long fingers wrapped around her throat. "Watch your tongue. I shall only take so much of it before I cut it out."

He released her and Cara staggered back, rubbing at her bruised neck. She coughed and said, "Try that again, and I'll kill you."

Kazan turned and stared at Janssen. "My friend, take my money now before I change my mind."

"Where are you taking me?" Cara asked him.

"Pripyat, my dear. You'll enjoy it immensely. The weeds are simply lovely this time of year."

––––––

Interpol, Brussels
Belgium

"What are we looking at?" Thurston asked the man beside her as they studied the large screen before them.

His name was Victor Denis. He was a man in his later thirties who ran Interpol's special operations unit in Belgium. While the operations team was in Antwerp, the small Bravo element was in Brussels as his guest. He said, "What you are seeing is a picture from one of my men's body cams. They are holding out the back of the property. Charges have been laid ready to breach the back fence. Your team is in our armored breaching truck along with more of my men. Your team leader has overall command of the assault because it is your person inside. Once the truck hits the gate, then the back fence will be blown."

Thurston nodded. "Can we see them?"

"Of course," Denis said, turning to one of his computer techs. "*Breng het andere team naar voren.*"

The picture on the large screen split and another body cam picture came online. "This one is from your man. The leader."

"Why can't I hear anything they're saying?"

"My people can," he assured her. "Once they breach, then everything will be on speaker."

"Thank you for your help with all this, Victor," Thurston said to him. "We appreciate everything you've done and are doing for us."

He smiled at her. "If it means we can get rid of this blight on our society, then I would not hesitate to do it many times over."

"What about Janssen's men? How many?"

"Our best count is seven. There are three on the outside of the house and another four inside. Plus, Janssen himself. All of his bodyguards are ex-military, SFG."

"When do we go?"

Denis offered her a headset. "Just say the word."

Thurston took it and placed it on her head. It felt like an old friend coming home, and a sense of calm replaced the nerves she'd been feeling. Moving the arm mic in front of her mouth, she said, "Reaper One? Bravo. Copy?"

———

Joint Assault Team
Antwerp

"Reaper One? Bravo. Copy?"

"Copy, Bravo."

"Are you ready that end?"

Kane looked around the confined space of the armored breaching truck. Across from him sat Brick and Axe, while Arenas was seated beside Kane himself. They were dressed in full tactical gear, and each wore body cameras, a stipulation of the Interpol agent in charge.

Three other shooters from Interpol Special Police were in the vehicle as well. These too were decked out in full tactical gear. One of them noticed Kane looking and gave him the thumbs up.

"Roger, Bravo, we're good to go."

"Copy. On my mark, the power will be cut, and you will go. Three, two, one, execute."

The truck lurched forward as the driver hit the gas. Having an automatic transmission, he didn't have to worry about changing gears, and the vehicle picked up speed almost instantly. Kane said into his comms, "Once we breach, call your kills. We know there's seven for sure, so we want them all accounted for."

"Copy that."

Everyone dropped their NVGs into place just before the truck hit the gates. The momentum of the heavy vehicle blew through the reinforced steel barriers with ease and roared along the drive until it reached the turnaround. Once there, the driver braked, and the truck slid to a stop.

As soon as it ceased moving, the back door opened and those within moved with practiced precision.

Kane immediately went left while behind him, Brick moved right and swept around that side. The rest of the assault team exited the truck and took up their positions. The NVGs painted everything before them green, the laser sights on Reaper Team's HK416s standing out in stark contrast.

Movement to Kane's left signaled the arrival of the first guard. The laser sight fell upon the man's chest, and Kane squeezed the trigger twice. The recoil of the carbine slammed back into his shoulder, and the target jerked wildly, releasing a weapon which clattered to the ground. Kane said in a calm voice, "Tango down in the drive."

A weapon fired on the far side of the truck, and Brick said, "Second tango down in the drive."

Kane said, "Moving toward the house."

"Reaper One? Bravo. Team Two has breached and moving toward the rear door."

"Copy, Bravo."

As Kane cautiously approached the front door, Arenas fell in behind him. The Team Reaper leader was about to test the door when it seemed to explode in a shower of long splinters as bullets from within the house punched through it. Kane ducked and moved to his left. "Fuck me," he hissed, glad that he had his armor on. Arenas moved right, so they were either side of the shattered obstacle. "Brick?"

"On my way," the ex-SEAL said through his comms. He tucked himself in beside Kane.

"Put a flashbang in there so we can breach."

"Copy."

"Ready?"

"When you are."

Kane stared across at Arenas and said into his comms, "We're breaching. Carlos, get the door."

Arenas waited for a break in the firing and then stepped across and kicked the door open. Pulling the pin on the flashbang, Brick tossed it inside just as another burst of gunfire erupted from within.

The M84 detonated, and Kane wheeled around and into the doorway. He entered the reception area and saw the armed figure loom large in front of him. Two spaced shots put the man down. "One down in the reception."

Axe and Arenas moved up the stairs while Kane and Brick started to clear the ground floor level rooms. A figure appeared at the head of the stairs, but three accurately-placed shots from Arenas dealt with him quickly.

"Tango down on the stairs."

Once at the top, the two Team Reaper men separated left and right and started to clear the second-floor rooms.

Kane and Brick cleared the large living room before exiting it and moving across the foyer to another door.

"Tango down first bedroom."

Kane placed his hand on the knob, and the door sprang free of the jamb. He swung it wide and moved back so Brick could step through the opening. The flashes of a handgun split the darkness followed by the sharp crack of its reports. Angry lead hornets cut through the darkness alongside Brick's head, but the ex-SEAL never flinched. Instead, the laser sight reached out unerringly to the target, and he squeezed the trigger four times. The impacts flung the shooter backward, and he collapsed onto a sofa.

Coming along behind Brick, Kane moved to the right, ensuring that his line of fire was unobstructed, and he cleared that side of the room. A figure appeared before him, but this one was unarmed. "Get on the floor!" Kane shouted. "Now!"

The person obeyed, and the Team Reaper commander hurried forward, taking out a cable tie as he went. As he brought the man's hands around to fasten them, he heard Brick's voice say, "Room clear. Tango down in the study, one prisoner."

Kane said, "Give me a sitrep."

"Upstairs clear, Reaper," Axe said.

"Downstairs clear," an accented voice said in English.

"We're still missing one shooter outside," Kane snapped. "Where is he?"

Nothing.

"Bravo, copy?"

"Copy, Reaper One."

"Have the Interpol guys do another sweep outside."

"Copy."

"Carlos, copy?"

"Copy."

"Any sign of the package?"

"Negative."

"Fuck it," Kane swore savagely. "I want this whole building swept from top to bottom. Do it now. And let's get some power on."

———

Axe stepped through the study door and looked resignedly at Kane. He gave an almost imperceptible shake of his head, but the look combined with the slight head movement was sufficient to convey the message. Kane knew the outcome, and said into his comms, "Bravo, no sign of the package. She's not here."

Brick appeared behind Axe. "Not too fast, Reaper. Come and have a look at this."

Kane indicated Janssen. "Keep an eye on this asshole, Axe."

"Can I shoot him?"

"Not yet."

"You're no fun."

Kane followed Brick out into the foyer, and for the first time, noticed the large chandelier. "Who the hell has something like that in their home? I think they have delusions of grandeur."

"I know what you mean," the ex-SEAL said as he started up the stairs. "If I had something like that in my house, it would fall on my fucking head."

"What do you want to show me, anyway?"

"I found something in one of the bedrooms."

They continued to ascend the grand staircase and turned left at the landing, taking the corridor that veered in that direction until Brick stopped outside a door that stood ajar. "Look at this and tell me what you see."

Kane ran a well-trained eye over it and picked up what Brick was referring to. "The key is in the lock on the outside."

"Yes. So that got me thinking. We'd already searched this room once and found nothing. But I thought "stuff it", and I went to take a closer look."

He walked through the doorway, and Kane followed. Brick stopped and continued to speak. "I figured that Cara would assume that we'd do anything we could to find her. Turn over every stone. So, I did exactly that."

He crossed to where a framed picture hung on a wall, reached out and moved it aside. There, scratched into the wall was Cara's name and her USMC number.

"Son of a bitch," Kane breathed. "Good work, Brick."

"That feller we've got tied to the seat in the study is he –"

"Janssen."

"You figure he'll talk?"

"We're just about to find out."

Brick followed Kane back downstairs and into the study. Janssen looked arrogant, sitting on a chair under the watchful eye of two Interpol agents. Axe was nowhere to be seen. "Damn it, Axe, where are you?"

"I'm having another look around."

"Get back here now. Carlos, you too."

"Roger that."

The Team Reaper leader turned to the two Interpol officers and said, "You two out."

They gave him a confused look, and he repeated his order more forcefully this time. "Out, now."

"Reaper, what's going on?" Thurston asked.

"She was here," he replied and removed his body cam.

"Reaper, I've lost your feed."

Kane looked at Brick who did the same.

"Damn it, Reaper. What is going on? We've lost Brick now."

Axe and Carlos appeared through the doorway, and Kane pointed at his and Brick's cams. They nodded and removed theirs. Now Thurston was a little more than pissed, and her angry voice came over the comms. "Reaper, what the hell is going on?"

"Reaper Team going off comms."

"What? Don't you fucking dare, Reaper One!"

Kane killed the comms and turned to Janssen. He took a picture from his pocket and walked over to the chair. Without saying a word, he raised his right leg and planted a large boot fair in the middle of the drug boss' chest. The chair and man flipped backward, crashing onto the floor. Kane moved around and dropped a knee into Janssen's stomach, making him grunt. "Look at the picture, mother-fucker. I know she was here. Where is she now?"

Janssen set his jaw firm but said nothing.

Kane slapped him across the face, drawing blood from the corner of his mouth. "Where?"

"Fuck you."

This time Kane hit him with a closed fist. "Listen, you son of a bitch. I can do this all day."

Janssen spat blood on the floor and smiled, showing pink teeth. "Fuck you, American."

The M17 came into Kane's hand, and he pressed the barrel against the drug boss' head. "Last chance."

"Ease up, Reaper," Brick cautioned him.

Kane ignored him.

"Come on, Reaper, what the fuck, man?" Axe said. "Put the gun away."

"John," Carlos joined them. "We will find another way. We'll find her."

"Christ! Fuck!" Kane roared, removing the barrel from Janssen's head, who looked up and smiled at him. Kane's anger boiled over. The M17 drove forward butt first, and it hit the drug boss between the eyes, snapping the man's head backward before it lolled forward onto his chest. Kane whirled away and reactivated his comms. "Bravo Four, copy?"

"Copy, Reaper One."

"I need you to track down every camera within a kilometer of this place and see what you can come up with."

"What exactly am I looking for, Reaper?"

"I don't know."

CHAPTER 8

Somewhere Over Europe

Cara stared out the window of the Cessna Citation Latitude and down at the water-dotted landscape. It was verdant, and the morning sunlight made the lakes sparkle like jewels in a wonderous crown.

"It is the Masurian Lakes District," Aleksey Kazan said from behind her. "It's beautiful, isn't it?"

Cara ignored him and went back to staring straight ahead. They'd been on the plane for the past couple of hours since leaving Antwerp. Kazan had kept her at a warehouse in the city for the best part of twenty-four hours before transferring her to the airport where she was then loaded onto the plane.

"We should arrive in Belarus in about thirty minutes. Once there, you will be kept with the other girls and then taken to market."

"Like I'm some piece of meat?" Cara sneered.

"A valuable piece of meat, my dear."

"Don't fucking "My dear" me."

The plane flew on, and as Kazan had said, thirty minutes later, it touched down smoothly on an airfield on the outskirts of Homyel' in the south of Belarus.

When they disembarked, there were two SUVs waiting for them. Cara looked around at the well-kept hangars, the beautifully maintained tarmac, and the high-security fencing, and concluded that the airfield was privately-owned. She was placed in the first SUV, and Kazan joined her. They were driven through the busy city where the SUVs stopped outside a large building built in the Socialist Classicism style after World War Two, on the banks of the River Sozh.

From there, Cara was taken from the vehicle and escorted through automatic, sliding-glass doors into a grand foyer. It was obviously a hotel but one with a difference. The establishment had armed guards in the public areas, carrying AK-104s.

The small group walked over to a reception counter, and Kazan was greeted by a middle-aged man wearing glasses. "Good morning, Mr. Kazan. Your usual room is available, sir."

"Thank you, Ivan," Kazan said.

"How many nights will you be with us this time, sir?"

"Just the one. We leave for the Ukraine tomorrow."

"Yes, sir. Will you require any room service? Or ...," he looked at Cara. "... have you brought your own?"

Kazan smiled. "Send me Mischa. I have time for a little entertainment tonight. Maybe even dinner."

"I'll have your table set."

"Thank you."

Ivan passed over an electronic room key which Kazan placed in his pocket. Crossing the polished red granite floor toward a bank of two elevators, he noticed Cara taking in her surroundings and chuckled. "Do not worry about trying to escape. This hotel is unbelievably secure. All the armed guards are ex-Russian military. Ivan was once a Spetsnaz officer. The security system is one of the best, which is why I, and many others like me, stay here."

"You mean assholes?"

Kazan shook his head. "All I'm trying to do is be civil to you. But you keep throwing it back into my face."

"What's civil about trafficking women?"

"Suit yourself."

"My people will come for you. For me," Cara hissed.

Kazan shrugged. "Maybe."

"And Kane will kill you."

A smile returned to his face. "Who is this Kane? Is he some kind of super-hero?"

When Cara answered, it wasn't what he expected. "He's no super-hero. He's the "Reaper"."

Antwerp Belgium

The SUV rocketed towards the airport where a plane waited. Through his comms, Kane heard Thurston say, "You should arrive in Homyel' in two and a half to three hours. That'll put the time at just after eighteen hundred. You'll go in with as little noise as possible. Understood?"

"We'll do our best, Ma'am," Kane said, trying to reassure her. "What do we know about the hotel and Kazan?"

A breakthrough had come earlier in the afternoon when Swift managed to ascertain what had happened to Cara.

Although he couldn't work out who they were looking for. He reached out to Interpol who in turn went through several channels until a hit came back through British Military Intelligence.

The name BMI threw back at them was Aleksey Kazan. A well-known European people trafficker and arms dealer.

"Kazan usually travels with an entourage of four. All ex-military. He's worth a lot of money thanks to his business. Last year, he sold two hundred million dollars' worth of arms to the rebels in Sierra Leone for their little coup attempt. And that's just the tip of the iceberg. He also has a pipeline across Europe through which he runs girls and then sells them by auction. Interpol and British Military Intelligence have heard whispers that there is an auction coming up, but they can't be certain where it will be held."

"Surely they would have some sort of indication of the location because of previous ones."

"That's just it, he moves them around. France, Germany, Lithuania. Never in the same place twice in a row."

"So, we have to hope that they're still at the hotel when we arrive," Kane surmised.

"That's about it," Thurston said.

"OK. What can you tell us about the hotel?"

"That is something else. It was built just after the Second World War. But since then, it's been updated. Slick should be able to get you past all the electronic stuff, but it's the guards you'll need to worry about. All are heavily-armed and very well-trained."

"We sure don't pick the easy ones, do we?"

"No," Thurston agreed. "By the way, how are your team's parachuting skills?"

Kane's blood ran cold. He had a feeling that things were about to get a whole lot worse. "Why?"

"The only way to get you into the building is from the top. It's only about ten floors up, but you'll still have to hit it."

Fuck!

"Are you still there, Reaper?"

"Yes, Ma'am."

"Look, I know it's not ideal, but if you go in from below, you'll be up against it from the start."

"Just say we pull this off. What is our exfil plan?"

"There will be a dark blue BMW across the street from the hotel. The keys will be under the sun visor, and it will be unlocked. You get Cara, get in, and drive away."

"What time do we jump?"

"Twenty-two hundred."

"If we get there at eighteen hundred, and we jump at twenty-two hundred, what are we doing for the intervening four hours?"

"Circles. I'll call you back before you go."

Thurston signed off, and Kane let out a long sigh. "Fuck me."

"What is it?" Brick asked from the driver's seat.

"You don't want to know."

———

Homyel' Belarus

The man's complacency had cost him his life. He'd thought that Cara, being a woman, wasn't a threat. He'd found out the hard way when his neck had snapped like a dry twig. It was a mistake he'd never make again.

Cara leaned over the corpse and removed the handgun from its shoulder holster. It was an MP- 443 Grach. She checked the loads and then made her way towards the door. Kazan had gone out somewhere, leaving her with only the one guard. Opening the door, she slipped out into the hallway. Looking around, Cara saw the security camera immediately, its light flashing red indicating that it was operating.

"No going back now," she muttered to herself and began moving quickly along the luxurious carpet of the hallway toward the far stairs. Suddenly the stairwell door opened and a figure appeared. It was one of Kazan's bodyguards.

"Hey!" he shouted and went for his sidearm.

Cara brought the Grach up and put two bullets in the man's chest, moving toward him without hesitation as the sound of the gunshots rolled along the hallway with a deafening roar. She knew that the noise would have alerted someone and stepped over the fallen guard and into the stairwell.

They would be coming for her now, Cara was sure. The echo of voices and footsteps wafted up from below, and she waited until she could see them then leaned out into the void. The Grach bucked in Cara's hands and, compared to the hallway, the sound was a hundred times worse. Without the acoustic properties of the carpet to absorb the sound, the bare concrete bounced the sound from wall to wall. Her ears rang, making her wince. All noise from below was drowned out. Her way down was blocked, so the only choice seemed to be going back through the hallway and into the room, then maybe climb over the balcony.

She opened the door and saw two men armed with AK-

74s coming towards her. "Shit!" she cursed and slammed the door. Cara started up the stairs. It seemed to be the final option. The roof! And hope like hell there was a way down.

She took the stairs two at a time and soon reached the landing at the exit onto the roof. Cara tried the door and pushed. It swung open, and she rushed out onto the rooftop, glad to be out of the confinement of the stairwell. Apart from a couple of large air-conditioning units, the roof was bare.

Cara ran to the nearest ledge and peered over the side. Her head spun at the vertical drop. She stepped back and ran to another ledge. It was the same. So too the third and fourth.

Tears of frustration sprang into her eyes. There was no way down. Whirling about, she ran back towards the stairwell door and had just about reached it when it opened. Kazan, along with several armed men, stepped out onto the roof. By the look on his face, he wasn't impressed with her antics.

"There is nowhere for you to go," he told her. He pointed at the Grach. "Give me the gun."

Cara hesitated. "If you give me the gun, I'm willing to overlook the fact that you have killed some of my men. If not, then I guess you can work out what will happen."

With shoulders slumped in resignation, Cara dropped the Grach to the rooftop. *Live to fight another day.*

"Good. Now we are leaving."

Surprise registered on Cara's face. "Why?"

"It would seem that we are to have visitors, and I would rather not be here when they arrive."

A flicker of hope crossed her face. "What visitors? Is it my team?"

"You don't need to worry about that. All that should

concern you is the auction the day after tomorrow. Now, let's go."

———

Team Reaper C-17
Somewhere Above Homyel' Belarus

"Two minutes to jump!"

C-17 pilot Jack Skipper's voice filled the headset fitted snugly over Kane's ears. Upon hearing the call, he looked across at the loadmaster, Ken Hellier, who confirmed the message with hand signals. Kane pressed the talk button for his comms and said, "Time to go, people."

They all stood up and shuffled toward the rear of the plane. Each one was fully-clad in black; fatigues, parachutes and tactical vests. The ramp began to lower with a whir. All Kane could think about was the conversation he'd had with Thurston just thirty minutes ago which had opened with, "They know you're coming."

"Jesus H Christ, how?" Kane had breathed into his comms.

"A leak from Interpol. It's plugged now, but we're not sure how much they know."

"That's just fucking great. We can say goodbye to Cara. They will have moved her by now for sure."

"We don't know that. But even if she's not, we may be able to get a lead on where the next auction is. I'll let Slick loose and have him see what he can turn up. At the moment, all we're seeing is a security team at a high level of readiness."

"There goes our quiet infil."

"Yes, I suggest you pack accordingly. But *try* not to let it get out of hand. The extract will still be the same."

"Copy that."

"I'll be in touch before you jump."

"Copy. Reaper One out."

Now they were about to leap from the plane at ten thousand feet, and Thurston still hadn't checked in.

"One minute!"

"Reaper One, this is Bravo, copy?"

"Copy, Bravo."

"As you suspected, they moved Cara. Slick was able to back through the security feed. The good news is that she's still alive."

"Was he able to track them at all?"

"Negative. He should be able to find them eventually, but ..."

"It could take a while," Reaper finished for her.

"That's affirmative."

"Nothing like live intel," Kane said.

"Roger that," Thurston said. "It's your call. The rooftop is clear, and once you touch down, Slick can take over the security feed and talk you through it if need be."

"Wait one, Ma'am."

Kane called the others to gather around him. "Listen up. The package has left the building."

"Ahh, Fuck!" Axe growled. "What now?"

"We can scrub the mission, or we insert and gather intel."

"What intel?" asked Brick.

"Where they might have taken Cara."

The ex-Seal nodded.

"Amigo," Arenas said, "I have a feeling there is something else."

"They know we're coming."

Suddenly the jump light changed to green, and the jumpmaster called out. "Hey, what the hell are you guys doing?"

Kane stared at his men, waiting for them to make a decision. Axe nodded. "Fuck it. Let's go."

"Yeah, do it," Brick said.

"Carlos?"

"No." They stared at him, and the Mexican smiled. "I'm just fucking with you. Let's go."

"All right," Kane said. "Let's do it."

All four men shuffled down the ramp and fell into oblivion.

———

Homyel' Belarus

"Bravo, all Reaper callsigns down and accounted for, over."

"Copy, Reaper One, good luck."

The team had made it without incident, touching down one after the other in close order. They discarded their parachutes and hid them behind a large air-conditioning tower.

"Bravo Four to Reaper One. Copy?"

"Copy, Bravo Four."

"You'll find the entrance to the building towards the northeast corner. That will lead you into the stairwell. I can see two guards on the other side of the door. I have control of the security feed, so no one knows you're here."

"Copy, Bravo Four."

Kane led the way across the roof, his suppressed HK416 up at his shoulder, ready to fire. Originally, the plan had been to just use their sidearms. However, that had all changed when the call had come through that their visit was no longer going to be a surprise. It was good planning that had the plane stocked with weaponry for all occasions should the need arise.

The team stopped at the door, and Kane whispered into his comms, "Bravo Four? Reaper One. We're at the door. Where are the tangos, exactly? Over."

"Directly at your twelve o'clock, Reaper One."

"Copy."

He signaled Arenas to come forward and said, "We're going to shoot through the door and then breach."

The Mexican nodded and raised his 416. Kane followed suit and spoke softly into his mic. "Three, two, one, execute."

Both carbines spit bullets through the door, burrowing into the flesh on the other side. Slick's voice came over the comms, "Both tangos are down, Reaper One."

"Copy. Breaching."

Kane went through first and secured the landing while Arenas secured the head of the stairs. Brick and Axe carried on down to the next landing where the stairs doubled back and down.

The team leader checked both downed men then stood back up. "Bravo, entry secure."

"Copy, Reaper One."

"Reaper One, this is Bravo Four. I suggest you go down to nine and then traverse to the other stairwell. You've got tangos outside the door on eight."

"Copy, Bravo Four. We're moving."

With Brick on point, they continued down to the next

floor and halted outside the door. "Bravo Four, we're at nine."

"Copy. The hallway is clear on the other side of the door."

Brick opened the door, and Axe stepped through the opening with his 416 at shoulder level. Suddenly, down below, a door slammed, and the echo reverberated up through the concrete canyon. They all halted, Arenas swinging around to cover the stairs. When no one appeared, they continued into the hallway.

The carpeted corridor muffled the sound of their boots. From within one of the rooms, the unmistakable sound of shooting and yips of someone watching a western on a television overrode the hum of the air-conditioning. Up ahead, a door opened, and a man appeared. Axe's red dot sight settled on him, and his finger prepared to stroke the trigger, sending the man on a one-way trip to the promised land. However, the man turned right instead of left and was walking away from them.

Axe let out a sigh of relief which caught in his throat when the man stopped and turned back.

"Oh, shit!" the ex-recon marine blurted out and fired two shots. The man dropped in the middle of the hallway, and Axe said, "I hope he was a bad guy."

"Everyone here is a bad guy, Axe," Kane told him.

As they approached the far door to the stairwell, Swift came back over the comms. "The stairwell beyond the door is clear, Reaper One. Head down to the second floor where you'll have to do the same again."

"Copy, Bravo Four."

They emerged from the ninth floor and started down the stairs. They'd passed six and were about to hit five when the comms crackled to life. "Reaper Team, hold. I say again, hold."

They stopped and took up a defensive pose. Kane waited a few heartbeats before Swift's voice came back online. "There are two armed tangos coming up the stairs towards you, and two moving towards your position from the sixth-floor. Looks like they know you're there."

"Copy that. How far away are the ones on six?"

"They're about at the door."

"Roger," Kane replied and then, "Let's go back up to six."

They hurried up the stairs to the sixth-floor landing, and Kane said, "Sitrep, Bravo Four."

"They're a few meters away from the door now."

"Copy."

The team leader raised his 416 and put a full mag through the door and into the hallway beyond. "How about now?"

"Tangos down, Reaper One."

Kane opened the bullet-riddled barrier, and Brick stepped through, checking the two downed men while Axe kept moving. Kane said, "Secure us an elevator."

"Roger."

By the time they reached the elevator, Axe had already summoned one, and it was on its way to their floor. When the doors slid open, they were faced with an empty space. "Everyone in."

The four of them got into the car, and Axe said to Kane, "This is a fucked idea, Reaper."

"They won't be expecting us to use it," he pointed out.

"Or they'll shoot us as soon as the doors open."

"There is that."

"Reaper One? Bravo Four. I have a sitrep, over."

"Send, Bravo Four."

"You have two guards just outside the elevators, and another two near the main entrance. When you get off that thing, they will be at your twelve o'clock. Another is near the main desk."

"Is that all?" Kane asked.

"Isn't that enough? Listen, there's also a clerk behind the counter. He looks to be strapped, too. However, you'll need him alive. He's probably the only guy who can give you any information."

"Copy that, Bravo Four," Kane acknowledged. "You guys get that?"

"Yeah," said Axe. "Don't kill the dude behind the desk."

"Carlos and I will clear left and right. Brick, Axe, you clear the two at twelve. That leaves the two at the counter. One guard and the clerk. Once we're secure, we get the son of a bitch into the car. We won't waste time, but will question him after."

The elevator passed one and then slowed to a halt on the ground floor. The bell went ding, and the doors slid open. Arenas and Kane moved through the doors at virtually the same time. The Mexican dropped the guard on the left with two shots, and Kane did the same to the surprised one on the right. The spent casings were still bouncing on the floor when Axe and Brick exited the elevator. Their suppressed 416s coughed twice, and the two guards at twelve o'clock fell to the hard floor.

Kane swept right towards the counter and saw the guard there begin to move. The AK-74 in the man's hands came up, but before he could depress the trigger, a 5.56 round smashed into his chest.

Clattering to the floor, the guard's weapon was quickly followed by his body. The man behind the counter brought up a handgun and began to take aim. Kane shouted, "Put the weapon down!"

Then the others joined in. "Put the weapon down! Put it down!"

The man hesitated. Then a muscle in his face twitched, and Kane knew he was about to fire. The team commander reacted instantly and moved his aim ever so slightly. The 416 coughed, and the slug punched into the would-be shooter's shoulder. Grunting, the handgun fell from his useless fingers. Brick moved forward and cable-tied the struggling man's wrists. "Is he OK, Brick?" Kane asked.

"He'll live."

"Right, get him up before the rest of them come down," Kane snapped. "Bravo Four, how's it look outside?"

"Apart from traffic, you're good to go."

"Copy, extracting package now. Let's move out. Axe, Arenas, secure our ride across the street. Remember, you're looking for a dark BMW."

"Roger that."

"Reaper One? Bravo, copy?"

"Copy, Bravo."

"There will be a helo on the outskirts of Homyel', ready to fly you and your package out of Belarus. I'll send you the coordinates. We'll meet you at the safehouse in Warsaw, where we can question him."

"Copy, Ma'am. See you there."

Kane and Brick hurried outside into the bright sunshine on the sidewalk and started across the road with their prisoner. The others had found their ride, and Kane winced when he saw Axe in the driver's seat. "Put him in the trunk," he said as he pressed the release mechanism.

The latch gave with a click, and as Brick went to lift the lid, it glided gracefully up of its own accord. He marveled at it before shoving the unwilling man inside. Kane asked, "He won't bleed out before we get to the RV, will he?"

"Nope, I put some clotting powder on the wound before we brought him out."

The trunk closed softly and locked, and they opened their doors and climbed in. "Get us out of here, Axe. Preferably in one piece."

"Are you saying you don't like my driving, Reaper?"

"That's an affirmative."

"I'm hurt," the ex-recon marine said, flooring the accelerator.

CHAPTER 9

Pripyat Ukraine
   Two Days Later

The SUV bumped over a decayed street which was slowly
being reclaimed by nature. The deteriorated asphalt was a
maze of grasses and saplings growing from the wide cracks.
In every direction, scarred buildings that had fallen into
disrepair were a stark reminder of the catastrophic events of
over thirty years ago when the Chernobyl Nuclear Facility
had gone into meltdown. It had taken until the day
following the disaster for authorities to evacuate Pripyat,
and by then most of its citizens had been irradiated to some
extent. Although no ongoing illnesses had been recorded
after the explosion and subsequent meltdown, there was a
spike in thyroid cancer which some attributed to the Chernobyl facility.

Once a buzzing metropolis of almost fifty thousand resi-
dents, the only people Pripyat saw these days were tourists
come to satisfy some macabre pleasure at seeing and

photographing the rotting corpse, silent and eerie, left to nature to take its course.

They drove past the old amusement park where the large wheel stood decomposing, stationery and rider-less over the intervening years. Beside Cara, Kazan noticed her looking out the window. "It is a special place, Pripyat."

"It's a reminder of the horrors and devastation the human race has wreaked upon the planet," Cara said bluntly. "Also, it shows you what can happen if you fuck up."

"True," Kazan allowed. "And if you're worried about radiation, we are relatively safe."

"I wasn't worried. I figure that if you're willing to risk your ass coming here, then it must be safe."

He smiled at her. Up ahead, the lead SUV pulled into what used to be the carpark of a large hotel. Cara noticed other vehicles within the grounds, and a quick mental count came out at twenty. "I must be popular to warrant this kind of turn out."

"As much as I would like to agree with you, sadly I must say that this auction has another, much larger attraction."

The SUVs came to a halt, and they climbed out. There was a slight chill in the morning air, and Cara shivered involuntarily. She looked over at Kazan and asked, "What kind of attraction?"

He shrugged. "Something that many here would pay most dearly for."

"Such as?"

"Nineteen ninety-three, Bosnia. A little incident between a Russian bomber and an American F-16. They clipped wings and crashed in a region that was in the grip of some very savage fighting. By the time peacekeepers made it to the crash site, a lot of things had been stripped from both planes. Including something of high importance on the Russian bomber. So important that the Russian high command was willing to risk losing a Spetsnaz team to retrieve it. Dropped in almost straight away, they worked their way to the crash site and secured it. But before they could do anything, they were attacked by soldiers. Out of twelve Spetsnaz men, only one survived. And that man was Ivan."

"Ivan?"

"Yes."

"What was so important that nineteen lives were just thrown ..." Cara's voice trailed away into silence. Her eyes darted to Kazan in a questioning glance, but her expression told him she already knew the answer. He nodded.

"What, the plane was carrying a nuclear weapon?"

Another nod.

"And you found it."

———

"Oh, this just keeps gets better," Axe muttered. "We get eyes on Cara, and then this just falls into our laps from a great fucking height."

Kane and Axe slid away from the rooftop edge, taking the listening device with them. The team had infiltrated Pripyat the previous evening after Ivan had given up the auction site. Having obtained permission from the Ukrainian government, they were able to set up a safehouse for Bravo to operate from with two elements of the Ukrainian military liaising. One of them, a general called Dmytro Borisov, was with Thurston at the safehouse. The second, a captain called Klara Ivanov, had infiltrated Pripyat with Team Reaper.

Kane pressed his transmit button, "Bravo, did you get that last?"

"Copy, Reaper One. Wait, out."

Kane sat up, looking around at the others. All had concerned expressions on their faces. He said, "You're all experienced enough to know what they're going to say next."

Brick nodded. "They're going to order us to secure the nuke at all costs. I can't believe that shit Ivan knew about the nuke and never said anything."

"That's right," Kane conceded. "Any suggestions?"

"We need eyes on the inside," Arenas said. "Maybe we can twofold the mission by extracting Cara and securing the weapon."

"You've seen the armed men going in and out. What's our latest count?"

"Twenty, maybe," Axe said.

"We're not exactly dressed to be infiltrating anywhere," Kane pointed out.

Ivanov asked, "What about the cars? These people have come a long way to be here. They must have clothes in them, surely."

"Only one way to find out. Axe, go and see what you can come up with."

Axe laid down his M110A1 and hurried across the rooftop. Just then, Kane's comms crackled to life. "Reaper One? Bravo, over."

"Copy, Bravo."

"You need to secure the nuclear weapon. This must be priority number one. If that gets out into the world, then who knows where it will end up. Do you understand? Cara is secondary."

"Yes, Ma'am, we're working on it right now."

"I'm sorry, Reaper."

"Yes, Ma'am. Reaper One out."

Axe returned ten minutes later with the total sum of one suit and one opal green dress and a pair of silver sling-backs. Arenas looked at the dress and said, "That will look beautiful on you, my friend, although it might clash with your eyes."

"Fuck you."

Kane stared at Ivanov. "You willing to do this?"

She nodded. "Yes."

"Thank you. How big is that suit?"

"I think it was worn by a frigging midget," Axe growled as he held it out.

Kane passed it over to Arenas. "Looks like you're it, my friend."

The Mexican gave a wry smile. "If any of you tell my wife that I accompanied a beautiful *senorita* on a date, I'll have your *cojones*."

"Go downstairs and get ready. Get the earwigs from the pack and give one to Klara."

After they disappeared, Brick said to Kane, "This here is a good overwatch position, but if they get into trouble, we need to be closer."

"I agree," Kane allowed. "Bravo Four, copy?"

"I'm right here, good buddy," Swift came back using his best truck driver impersonation.

The team leader saw Axe and Brick shake their heads. Brick snorted and said, "That is just shit, man."

"I don't know I thought it was pretty good. You know, almost Convoyesque."

"Oh, no man. You're not even close."

"Slick, do you have a secondary way into this place for us?" Kane asked, interrupting the banter.

"There should be a back door. There's always a back door ... and yes, sir, it's right there."

"Where?"

"Around the back."

"Damn it, Slick."

"If you hook around the east side, you can't miss it, Reaper. From the schematics that I have, it should take you through the kitchen. There is an old service elevator in there so you might be able to make use of it. The auction is being held in a large hall within an old conference center. It has a second-floor balcony running around it, which should make a good OP for you."

"Copy that."

"Axe, keep an eye on things. Brick and I'll be back in a moment."

They found Arenas and Ivanov adjusting themselves. Kane was taken aback at how good the Ukrainian Captain looked. Her black hair was down, and the dress hugged her lithe form like a silicone glove, accentuating all her curves. "What do you think? The shoes are a bit big, but I still think that they suit the outfit better than my boots."

He stared at her and opened his mouth to speak, but Arenas cut him off. "He thinks you are a picture of beauty."

She smiled, seeing that Kane was momentarily embarrassed by the words. Kane grumbled something and then said, "Bravo Four, are you still there?"

"I'm here ... ah, copy, Reaper One."

"We're going to need a backstop for Carlos and Captain Ivanov. I was thinking that seeing as he's Mexican, we could go down the cartel line?"

"Copy, Reaper. Working on it now. It'll just take a few minutes."

"Roger that," Kane acknowledged. He then said to Arenas, "You two need to get a story straight in your head."

"We'll work on it now."

"Good. Once Slick gets back to you with his backstop you go in. Brick and I are going to infil now. Good luck."

———

The man tossed an armful of colorful fabric on the floor and said, "Put these on."

Eight young women shuffled forward, picking through the dresses from the pile. Cara stood back and watched as they pawed over the jumble.

"Aren't you going to pick one?" a heavily-accented British voice said to her. Cara stared at the slim blonde and saw apprehension in her eyes. "They don't like it when we don't do as they say."

"Where are you from?"

"Suffolk in England."

"How did they get you?"

"I was at a club in France when I was drugged and taken."

"What's your name?"

"Kelly. What about you?"

"I'm Cara. They took me from America."

"Really?"

"In a way. Listen, we need to get out of here."

"How can we? There are so many men with guns. You've seen them."

"We'll work something out."

The door opened, and the same man reappeared. He looked around the room and picked out a young woman who'd already changed into an opal green dress. "You. Come."

She shook her head. "No, no, no, no ..."

She screamed out loud as the man took her roughly by the arm and began dragging her towards the door.

"Hey, asshole," Cara shouted at him, "let her go."

She took a step forward but stopped suddenly when he produced a gun and pointed it in her direction. "Stop, bitch."

Cara halted and watched on helplessly as the man and the struggling woman disappeared through the doorway. The heavy door closed with a loud bang. She said, "It looks like it has started."

"Oh, no."

———

Getting in was easier than expected. Maybe it was because of where they were. Who knew? But within minutes, Kane and Brick were inside the hotel and navigating the back hallway towards the kitchen. The air had a pungent musty smell to it, and the paint on the concrete walls had long ago started to peel away, forming small piles of flaky color on the dusty floor.

They reached the large kitchen and found it to be in much the same state as the hallway. Thirty years of dirt and debris was scattered across the floor. Wall tiles lay shattered where they'd fallen after their glue had given way. Previously white appliances were now covered in orange rust, and here too the walls shed huge flakes of paint like a giant with dandruff. An island bench where meals had been prepared was covered in dirt and bird shit, and external pipes had rusted through.

They found the service elevator and forced the door open. Inside the industrial sized space was much like everything they'd seen since entering; dirt-caked and decayed. "I hope the way up is manageable," Brick said.

"Let's find out."

They lifted the panel in the ceiling of the car and looked up. The shaft above them was dark and gloomy and filled with dusty spider webs. Kane lifted himself up and looked around. Behind him, Brick started to do the same, and Kane turned back to pull him up. The elevator lurched, and for a moment, it felt as though the cable would give way. "Start climbing before this thing kills us. Watch out for spideys, too."

Fighting their way through the cobwebs, they scaled the framework until reaching the first floor. Not a substantial distance as such, but given the state of the shaft, the journey was still fraught with danger.

After prying the doors apart, they stepped out onto a grime-covered carpet. While Kane swept left, Brick covered their right. Kane said into his comms, "Reaper One and Five are on the first floor."

"Copy, Reaper One," Swift replied. "If you go to your right, you should find what you're looking for."

"How's that backstop going?"

"Finishing it up as we speak."

Kane and Brick moved to their right and soon came to a door. Kane tried the handle, and the door clicked open. Going through the door was like being transported into a different world. The grand hall had been cleaned up, painted, and whatever its source, there was power. Kane figured it had to be solar.

"Good Christ," Brick whispered.

Brick and Kane edged forward to a position where they

could see almost everything below. The auction was already underway with a girl standing on a stage, a man beside her taking bids. The Team Reaper commander said, "Get pictures of everyone you can, Brick, and send them back as you go. Especially the girls, and if possible, those who buy them. With a little luck, we can ID them and get the poor buggers back."

"Copy that," Brick acknowledged and then spoke softly into his comms. "Bravo Four? Reaper Five. Copy?"

"Copy, Reaper Five."

"We're in position. I'm about to start relaying happy snaps to you. Some will be of the girls these guys are selling. The rest are their buyers."

"Roger that. Ready when you are."

While Brick started taking photos, Kane kept up surveillance on those coming and going. Ten minutes after they'd arrived, his comms crackled to life once again. "Reaper Three about to enter target."

"Copy."

———

Arenas and Ivanov approached the front door of the hall and were stopped by two men armed with AK-74s. The biggest of the two stepped across to block their path and growled in heavily-accented English, "Who are you?"

The Mexican's hard stare was designed to give the man the impression that he wasn't used to being questioned. Once that was established, Arenas said, "Montero. Chihuahua Cartel."

"Who's the whore?"

The Mexican's eyes sparked with fire. "You are one word away from death, my friend. You insult my wife in such a manner, back home, I would not only kill you but your family as well. And their family, and their family's family. Do you understand me?"

The man's expression never changed. "Where's your invitation? I need to see it."

Arenas patted down the suit in a fake search and then shrugged. "I do not have it."

"Then, you do not enter."

Ivanov stepped casually forward and grabbed the man by the crotch. She applied sufficient pressure to make the color of the guard's face change. Leaning in close, she hissed in a low voice, "First you call me a whore, and now you doubt my husband's word. You have exactly five seconds to make this right, or I will tear off your balls and give them to Mr. Kazan as a present."

The man swallowed hard and, in a strained voice, said, "Let me check the list."

Ivanov let him go and stepped back, adjusting her dress demurely. The man checked a tablet he had been holding and after a moment said, "Yes, you are here. Go in."

Arenas and Ivanov entered the hall, taking in everything that Kane and Brick had seen earlier. Ivanov said, "This is amazing."

"Reaper Three, we have eyes on you."

"Copy."

They walked through the crowd to where the auction was taking place. Standing just behind the first row, Arenas studied the young lady on stage. He whispered into his comms, "They're drugging the girls."

"That must be how they keep them subdued," Kane theorized.

Beside Arenas, Ivanov felt a hand slide up the back of her thigh and cup her butt cheek, naked below the smooth fabric. Standing behind her was a thin man dressed in a suit, a leering smile spread across his face. Beside him was a woman dressed in a short black dress with an extremely low-cut neckline, her décolletage and most of her breasts exposed. His other hand was beneath her dress without eliciting any reaction.

The man jiggled his eyebrows in a suggestive fashion. Ivanov smiled casually and reached out, grasping his erection through his designer pants. The man closed his eyes, fully expecting her to pleasure him, but instead, the Ukrainian Army captain twisted savagely, and the man let out a scream of agony, immediately withdrawing both wandering hands which gingerly covered his manhood.

All eyes immediately turned to him; the excruciating pain etched on his face. On the stage, the man next to the girl signaled someone, and two armed men pushed through the crowd and seized the man. Then, while painfully protesting his innocence in the matter, the man was dragged towards the door.

"You need to play nice with the natives, Captain," Kane said. "We don't need the attention."

"He shouldn't have grabbed my ass."

"Remind me not to do it then," he shot back with an amused smile.

Ivanov stifled a grin and went back to scanning the crowd around her. Her eyes lingered on a bald man and then moved once more. "I have Khasan Umarov in the building."

"Say again, Captain?" Thurston said.

"I have eyes on Khasan Umarov. He is at my three o'clock."

"Get me a picture, Bravo Five."

"Ma'am."

Khasan Umarov was a Chechen separatist wanted throughout Europe for multiple bombings. His last was in Russia where a government official and thirty civilians had been killed. "No surprises for guessing what he's here for," Kane said in a low voice.

"Reaper One, we've filtered through some of these photos, and it is veritable who's who of the dark side. I wouldn't be surprised to see Darth Vader. There is Hwan from North Korean Office 39, Kevin O'Connor from that new IRA splinter group, The New Dawn. Tony Hancock, the British arms dealer, and, get this, Krystal Meth, an Australian who acts as a broker between all the Middle East terror groups. I really could go on all day the way my computer screen is lighting up."

"All here for the nuke," Kane said.

"That's about it."

Kane looked at Brick. "You're the SEAL you have any suggestions?"

"How about we find the nuke?"

"Is that it?"

"That's all I've got. They've got to have it somewhere close."

Kane nodded. "Carlos, Klara, time for some recon. See what you can find."

"Copy."

"Reaper One, we may have a problem."

"Go ahead, Bravo."

"General Borisal has dispatched a company of his troops to your position."

Kane cursed under his breath. "If they show up here there's no telling what might happen to the nuke, Ma'am."

"I agree. That's why I'm telling you that you have thirty mikes to find and secure the damned thing."

"Copy that, Ma'am."

Suddenly down below, the man on the stage called out, "It is time for the next item on our list!"

"Reaper," Brick whispered urgently.

Kane looked down and saw the woman stepping up onto the stage. It was Cara. "Bravo, we have eyes on our package."

"The nuke, Reaper One?"

"No, Ma'am. Reaper Two."

"You have a new mission, Reaper," she reminded him. "Stay on it."

"Damn it, General, I can almost touch her."

"Stick to the mission, Reaper One. That's an order!"

"*Fuck!*" he hissed fiercely.

They observed in silence as the price rose phenomenally. Finally, the last bid in, the hammer fell, and Cara was sold at two million dollars. As they watched on, a man with dark hair and wearing a charcoal suit came forward to claim her. Kane said to Brick, "Did you get a photo?"

"Yeah, it's on its way to Slick."

"Did she look drugged to you?"

He hesitated.

"Brick?"

"Yeah, I think so."

Kane remained silent and watched them leave. Beside him, Brick said, "Is there any way you can track them from here, Bravo Four?"

"Not at the moment. The best I can do is work out who the purchaser is and track him from that. Sorry."

"Victim of circumstance, my friend. It's not your fault."

The next girl was brought out and put on the stage. This one was clearly drugged, her head lolling to the side as she swayed on the spot. Kane ground his teeth together and said, "Reaper Three, any sign of that nuke yet?"

"Wait one."

There was a long pause, and then Arenas' voice came back saying, "Affirmative, Reaper One. I have the location of the device."

"Are we able to extract it?"

"That could be a problem."

CHAPTER 10

Pripyat, Ukraine

"That could be a problem," Arenas said as he stared at the sight before him.

"What kind of problem?"

He was looking through a gap in the doorway at a silver suitcase secured within a clear, what he assumed to be a bulletproof encasement. Surrounding it were five men wearing tactical equipment, all armed with AK-74s.

"The package in question is a little more secure than we first expected. I'm about to send you a photo."

Arenas took a picture and hit send. It appeared on the devices of both Kane and Swift. "See what I mean?"

Kane glanced at his watch. They only had twenty minutes before the soldiers of General Borisov stormed into Pripyat and blew everything to hell. "Axe, you copy?"

"I'm still here, Reaper."

"I need a diversion. A big one."

"Any requests?"

"Something that goes boom. Do you still carry a grenade with you?"

"Never leave home without it. Give me ten mikes, and I'll see what I can do."

"That's about all you have; get at it."

"What's your plan, brother?" Brick asked Kane.

"We can't get the damned thing out of here, so we're going to have to secure it in place. If Axe can create a big enough diversion, it might get some people out of here, so we can get inside that room."

"I hope you're right."

"The only problem is that once we're inside, we'll be like rats in a trap. Everything relies on the Ukrainians getting here on time."

"Now that makes me feel a whole lot better."

"Not me," said a heavily-accented voice from behind them. "Stand up."

"Ah, fuck!"

———

"Reaper Three, Reapers One and Five have been compromised. Over."

"Copy, Bravo."

"Your priority is still the device, understood?"

"Yes, Ma'am."

Arenas walked back out towards the main hall where the auction was taking place. On the way, he said, "Axe, did you get that last transmission?"

"Yeah."

"How far away is the diversion?"

"About five mikes."

Arenas stepped into the auction room just as the two

Team Reaper men were paraded onto the stage. "You'd better hurry. I don't think they've got that long."

He watched one of the guards talk to the guy on stage and then disappear.

"Axe, keep an eye out."

"Copy."

Suddenly Ivanov appeared by his side. She touched his arm and said, "This is not good."

"Do you have a sidearm?"

"Yes."

"Look what we have here!" the auctioneer shouted to his audience. "Two intruders have come into our midst. Two Americans. One can only guess what they want here. Maybe they've heard about what we have on offer."

Someone with a thick Arabic accent called from the crowd, "I will give you ten million if you let me kill them!"

"Who is the man on stage, Bravo Four?"

"From our pictures, he is Kazan."

Kazan continued, "That is a very handsome offer. But I am almost certain that we can achieve a better result than that."

The man called out once more, "I will double that. Twenty million."

"Come on up here, my friend," Kazan said jovially. "You've just bought yourself a killing."

The man came free of the crowd, and Arenas recognized him instantly. After all, he'd seen the face many times on American television. Abu Samara, an Iranian-sponsored terrorist from the Iranian Martyrs. He had once been a colonel in the Iranian army, now one of the most wanted terrorists in the world; the man responsible for the bombing of a U.S. Embassy in Pakistan which killed fifty-four.

"Axe, you're out of time."

"That's good because I don't need any more."

There was a brief pause followed by the loud crump of something big blowing up. Then all hell broke loose.

———

To Axe, the plan was simple. Place the grenade, a few strategic shots, and boom, job done. He picked the cars clustered closest together. In the movies, the hero is often portrayed shooting the crap out of a car until it blows up, which makes for good theatre. Really, there was no proof whatsoever to back up the notion.

Now, settled back in behind the M110A1, he was about to squeeze off the first shot.

"Axe, you're out of time," came over the comms.

"That's good because I don't need any more."

The M110A1 had an optimum range of around eight hundred meters, but Axe was less than half that from his target, and the box magazine had twenty 7.62mm rounds just bursting to be released.

He squeezed the trigger, and the suppressed weapon slammed back into his shoulder. Shifting aim, he fired again. He did it five times. His first shot hit an Audi Coupe, his second an Aston Martin, the third was a petrol-powered Range Rover. His fourth shot punched a hole in a BMW.

The fifth shot, however, was the catalyst. Each previous shot had opened a hole in the vehicles' fuel tanks which had released their contents onto the ground. The final shot punctured the tire on a second Range Rover, deflating it instantly, dislodging the grenade which already had its pin pulled.

There were two explosions. The first was the grenade detonating, blowing the Range Rover apart and turning it into a burning, twisted mass of metal. The second was the ignition, by the first explosion, of the gasoline from the punctured fuel tanks on the other cars, turning them into an expensive and expansive fireball.

The explosions rocked the surrounding buildings, and Axe felt the heat of the blast from where he lay. "I hope you liked that, Reaper Three. It looks mighty pretty from out here."

———

Inside the large hall, things began to turn chaotic. The explosion had rocked the building, and the occupants were starting to panic. In alarm, a few women screeched, the sounds intermingled with various shouts from the men. Most of them made directly for the exit.

However, the Iranian wasn't about to leave before killing himself an American. Arenas saw him reach inside his Armani suit coat and pull a semi-automatic handgun. Samara began to bring it up, and Arenas produced his own M17, sighting and squeezing the trigger just before the Iranian fired, causing the terrorist to drop to the floor with a bloody hole in the side of his head.

Beside Arenas, Ivanov lifted the hem of her dress revealing a lithe, tanned thigh with a Fort-17 tucked into a thigh holster, as luck would have it, the opposite leg to the one that had been groped earlier. She pulled the weapon free and aimed center mass of an armed guard carrying an AK-74. Her first shot did as she designed it to do. The bullet struck the armor plating of the man's tactical vest, stopping him cold, even if it didn't kill him. She then raised her sights and fired again.

This time the slug ripped into the flesh just below the

guard's chin, doing irreparable damage. He fell to his knees, grasping at the mortal wound, blood flowing freely through his fingers despite his futile attempt to stem it.

Amid the confusion, Brick leaped down from the stage beside the dying guard and picked up the AK. It would have been so easy to cut loose with a hail of automatic fire and mow down all before him, but SEAL training had taught him otherwise. Instead, Brick picked his targets and eliminated them one at a time.

Against a surging tide, two guards fought their way through the main exit. Arenas saw them and fired his M17. One fell while the other spun with a flesh wound to the upper right arm.

Another guard appeared on the first-floor gallery. He opened fire, and bullet scars appeared on the floor all around Arenas before the misshapen slugs whined off across the hall. Someone screamed and fell, wounded in the legs from a couple of ricochets. The Mexican dived left to escape the zeroing gunfire. Ivanov fired twice from her Fort-17, and the shooter reeled back, dropping his AK over the balustrade and onto the main floor below.

Brick scooped the AK up and turned to Kane. "Here you go!"

He threw it to his team leader who caught it cleanly. But there was a look of alarm on Kane's face which told the ex-SEAL that there was some sort of issue. He spun around just in time to see Krystal Meth standing there, a crazy look in her eyes, and an FN Five-SeveN pointed at them.

The weapon bucked in her pale hand, and the bullet hit Brick in the chest, the armor plate of his vest taking the full force of it. He felt as though a horse had kicked him, and the big ex-SEAL dropped to his knees. Looking down, he saw the hole, felt wetness spreading beneath the vest. He looked up at her and saw a cold smile on her pale face. "How the fuck does that feel, mate?"

The bitch had shot him with an armor-piercing round which had blown straight through the plate. Now she was going to finish him off.

The Five-SeveN was now aimed at his forehead. In the fading light, Brick could just make out her trigger finger starting to whiten, and then everything went black.

Krystal seemed to be oblivious to everything happening around her. Maybe she was high or just didn't care, but her attention was fixated upon the man before her, and it appeared that nothing else mattered.

Two 7.62 rounds from the AK, which Kane held, punched into her chest between her mostly-exposed ripe-looking breasts. The deep V of her dress perfectly framing the twin dark holes that appeared in her once flawless flesh. They looked like a pair of black eyes which were starting to weep tears of deep red blood.

She looked down in amazement. Then with a, "Well, fuck me," she fell to the floor.

"Carlos! Brick's down! Get over here."

Kane dropped beside the downed man and checked him. He removed the damaged vest and saw all the blood beneath it on Brick's shirt. "Axe, get in here, now."

"Copy, coming to you."

"Reaper One? Sitrep, over."

"We have a man down. The bitch shot him with an armor-piercing round. It went straight through his vest."

"Copy. I'll get a medivac spun up."

"How far out are those troops?"

"Five mikes."

A hail of gunfire erupted from near the exit. Kane looked up and saw a guard standing there with an AK ripping round after round in their direction. Ivanov blew off the rest of her sidearm's magazine in the shooter's direction. He pulled back, and the captain took the opportunity to reload with a fresh one.

The guard leaned out to fire again but instead fell to the floor, Axe appearing behind him. "Stupid son of a bitch should've been watching his six."

He saw Brick on the floor, blood pooling about as it leaked from him at an alarming rate. "What do you need me to do, Reaper?"

"You and Carlos secure that fucking nuke."

"Copy that."

"What can I do?" Ivanov asked.

Kane took out a satchel of clotting agent and poured it into Brick's chest wound. Then he peeled a gauze pad from its packet and placed it over the blood source. "Hold this here. Put pressure on it."

She moved in beside him and pressed down hard to help stop the bleeding. Kane scooped up the HK-74 and said into his comms, "Bravo? Reaper One. How far out is that medivac?"

"Twenty mikes, Reaper One."

"Damn it. Does the Ukrainian unit have a medic with them?"

"Wait one."

About thirty seconds later, Thurston came back online. "That's a negative on the medic, Reaper One. What is your wounded man's condition?"

"He's critical, Ma'am. If we don't get help soon, he'll die."

"Sorry, Reaper One. We're doing the best we can."

"Well, do fucking better. Reaper One, out."

———

When Arenas and Axe arrived at the room where the nuke was being kept, the guards were frantically trying to get it out of the bulletproof case. However, they weren't the only ones within the vault room. Observing their progress was a rather anxious-looking British arms dealer.

Tony Hancock stood off to the side, handgun by his thigh, glancing back and forth from the device to the entrance of the room. He caught sight of the two Reaper men and brought the weapon sweeping up, blowing through half a magazine when it reached the top of its arc.

"Son of a bitch," Axe growled as fragments peppered his body. "He really wants that thing."

Arenas leaned around the corner of the opening and fired twice, scattering the guards. Axe cringed and shouted, "Watch the fuck where you're shooting, man. You don't want to hit the damned thing."

"The glass is bulletproof, Amigo."

"Yeah?"

"Yes."

"Well, what the fuck are we waiting for?"

Both men replaced half-filled magazines with fresh ones and looked at each other. Then with a sharp nod and a determined expression etched on their faces, they stepped into the room.

"How's he doing?" Kane asked Ivanov.

"Not good."

Kane's comms came to life. "Reaper, we've secured the nuke. Can Brick be moved?"

"Negative."

"Roger that, we'll come to you."

Kane kept sweeping the room and above for any new

threats while Ivanov continued to monitor Brick. Suddenly she gasped.

"What is it?"

"He's stopped breathing."

"Shit," Kane swore and moved in beside her. He checked for a pulse and found nothing. "Come on, you son of a bitch, don't do this now."

He raised his clenched fist and brought it crashing down upon the ex-SEAL's chest. Then he started performing compressions, counting them off in his head. "Klara, breathe."

"What?"

"Him. Breathe for him."

Ivanov leaned over Brick and tilted his head back. She opened his mouth to make sure his airway was clear, and then while pinching his nose, placed her mouth over his, sealing it, and then breathed deep into his lungs.

They had been working on him for a couple of minutes when Axe and Arenas appeared, bringing with them the suitcase nuke. "*Madre de Dios*," the Mexican breathed.

"Don't you let that asshole die on us, Reaper," Axe growled. "He's the only decent one among us."

"Reaper One, this is Angel Flight Lead, copy?"

"Come on, you son of a bitch, breath," Kane cursed, pushing harder on his chest.

"Reaper One, this is Angel Flight One, copy? Over."

"Come on, Brick, damn it!"

"Reaper One, this is Angel ..."

CHAPTER 11

Kiev, Ukraine

The heart monitor at the head of the bed beeped with monotonous regularity like a clock ticking off seconds through time. Kane sat beside the bed, his shoulders hunched over, head in hands, watching Brick's chest slowly rise and fall. IV lines, chest tubes, and wires seemed to be hooked up to or into every part of the ex-SEAL's body, keeping him alive.

The door behind him opened, and a voice asked, "How is he?"

Kane looked up and saw Doctor Rosanna Morales staring at him. She'd been flown out the day before to take over Brick's care. After nearly seventeen hours in the air, she looked about as good as could be expected.

She moved around to the foot of Brick's bed and looked at the tablet in her hands. Frowning, she read some more before saying, "He is a very lucky man. What you and the captain did saved his life."

Kane just nodded, suddenly aware of the strong disinfectant smell in the room. He'd been with Brick for the best part of three days, not wanting to leave until there was some sign of improvement in his man's condition. "The general told me to tell you that she wants you back at the ops center."

He gave a tired nod and spoke for the first time. "Is he going to live?"

"He's made it through the last three days so far. That's a good sign. Other than that, I don't know. That bullet did a bit of damage."

"Yeah."

Silence once more descended over the room, and, after a while, Morales said, "Aren't you going?"

"I don't know."

"I promise I'll take good care of him."

"I know that, Doc. It's just ..."

"Feels like you're leaving him behind?"

"That's it."

"Go, Mr. Kane. From what I understand, you have another important agenda to meet."

"Call me Kane or Reaper, Doc. Never mister."

"OK, Reaper. Time to go to work. Doctor's orders."

He rose from the chair and stretched all the kinks from his body. When he raised his arms, she noticed the M17 tucked in his belt. "Do you plan on using that thing in here?"

"Never can be too careful. Might be wise to get yourself one."

"You know my stance on guns."

"Yeah, I do. OK, Doc, take care of him. I'll go and see what the boss wants."

He started towards the door and then stopped. Turning

to look back at her, he said, "Hey, Doc. It's good to have you on board."

She gave him a soft smile. "Take care, Reaper."

———

Team Reaper Ops Center
Kiev

When Kane walked into the room, Thurston looked up from where she was standing next to Swift who was pointing at something on the screen. She said to him, "You look like shit."

"I feel that way too."

"Get yourself a shower and cleaned up. We have a briefing in fifteen minutes."

"What about?"

"Just do it, and you'll find out."

Kane went and showered, enjoying the heat of the water running down his back, then toweled off and dressed. He came back to the ops center, feeling remarkably refreshed and ready for whatever was coming in the briefing. Axe had his nose in a Clive Cussler book and looked up as Kane walked in. "You're still alive. I was starting to think all the rumors were true."

"Are you sure that book has enough pictures for you?"

"Ha, ha."

"What's up, anyhow?" Kane asked Axe.

"We have a line on Cara."

"Really? Where?"

"Italy."

Before he could ask another question, Thurston

appeared with Swift and Traynor. Following them was Arenas. The general asked Kane, "Did Axe fill you in?"

"Not quite."

"OK. Slick, bring everyone up to speed."

The red-headed computer marvel cleared his throat and started to outline what he'd learned. "It was hard, but I finally found out who our guy in the picture that Brick sent through, is. His name is Amando Bellandi."

The large flat screen they were using came to life, and a picture appeared on it. "This is said man. He has a string of high-class escort agencies and pours more money into the Italian Porn Industry than our own government puts into our armed forces."

"Is he Mafia?" Kane asked.

"No. This guy is much worse. The Mafia is scared of this guy. That's why they stay out of northern Italy. Milan seems to be the cutoff – an invisible border."

"Sounds like our kind of asshole," Traynor observed drily.

The picture changed to that of a broad-shouldered man with dark sunglasses. "This is Carlo Laurito. He used to be a Mafia enforcer. But he turned on his don when Bellandi asked him to. Cut his heart out and mailed it home to his wife. He's been working for Bellandi ever since."

The screen changed again, and a picture appeared of a lithe woman with long black hair, clad only in a skimpy bikini which barely contained her augmented breasts. Axe opened his mouth to speak, but his reaction was anticipated by his commander. "Stow it, Marine."

"Yes, Ma'am."

Swift continued. "This is his wife, Elettra. She runs his escort empire, with the flagship, as it is called in the business world, based in Milan."

"Where'd he meet her?" Kane asked.

"I knew you'd ask that," Swift said, and a DVD cover came up onto the screen with two semi-naked women on it with the title, *Escucha a Elettra gemir*. "It basically translates to Hear Elettra Moan."

"He married a porn starlet."

"Yes. It is a place to start. If our friend Bellandi has taken Cara to Italy, then it's a safe bet that they'll try to place her in one of their agencies there."

Thurston said, "We're all flying to Milan. I'm also bringing the rest of the team in. We need to find Cara before this all goes too far."

"What does Bellandi do while his wife is making out with the girls?" Kane asked.

"He runs one of Italy's biggest drug empires."

"How are we going to do this?"

"I'll set up Bravo in a safehouse, while you and Axe pose as tourists and check out the nightlife."

"You want us to go into one of them fancy whore houses, Ma'am?" Axe asked, surprised.

"It's the only way you'll gather intel. One of the girls will know something. I'd bet my last dollar that half of them were bought just as Cara was."

"If he's as bad as what you say, none of the girls are going to talk. They'll be too scared," Kane pointed out.

"Let's hope they're not. Wheels up in two hours."

"Ma'am, I have a question," Kane said.

"What is it?"

"Can I take Carlos to the brothel instead of Axe?" he asked, then stared at his friend. "At least he's married, and I won't have to worry about him doing something stupid."

"Hey, are you calling me stupid? I swear your constant lack of trust in me hurts my feelings."

"Axe will fit right in at the place. That's why I chose him. Pumped full of testosterone just like a teenager in a sorority house on a college campus."

Axe gave him his best shit-eating grin. "See. The boss trusts me."

Kane shook his head. "This is going to end in tears; I know it."

"It sure will be a pleasure."

Thurston rolled her eyes. "Work, Axe, not pleasure. You even go there; you'll probably catch something which will cause your little worm to shrivel and die."

His head snapped around, and he said to Kane, "Did she just say worm?"

"I think so."

"No, surely not."

"Yes, I think it was definitely worm. And a little worm at that."

"She is a cruel lady."

"She's an officer."

"That explains it then. It was still harsh."

"I thought so. Me, I'd have called it a grub."

"Reaper?"

"Yeah?"

"Fuck you."

"If you two are quite finished, go and get your shit together. Now."

"Yes, Ma'am."

Milan, Italy

. . .

The black-haired woman with the big tits threw the evening gown at Cara and snapped, "Put that on. You will need a shower too."

"What's it for?"

"You and a few of the other girls will be entertaining some very important people tonight."

"What if I refuse?"

"You won't," the woman said, sounding more than a little confident. "We have no use for girls who do not work."

Cara knew what her words meant and remained silent. *Just stay alive.*

She'd heard what had happened in the Ukraine. About the attack by foreign soldiers. About the capture of Kazan and the nuke. It made her wonder whether they'd been there watching while she'd been sold, and if so, why hadn't they rescued her or the other girls?

Cara was escorted to the shower where she washed her body and her hair, then wrapped herself in a towel as a final protest, before donning the dress when the guard threatened to dress her. Her hair and makeup were done for her like she was a movie star, and once she was ready, she almost didn't recognize the person in the mirror.

"There, Elettra will be happy with that," the makeup girl said.

"Who is Elettra?" asked Cara.

"The woman."

Before she could answer, the woman with the dark hair appeared again. Elettra nodded with satisfaction and said, "Good. Much better. The clients will be most satisfied with the offering tonight. Here take this."

Cara looked down at the outstretched hand and saw a little yellow pill. "What's that?"

"Something to make the night go a little smoother."

"I don't want it," Cara said, remembering the last time she'd been drugged in Pripyat.

"I wasn't asking."

Cara took the pill and placed it into her mouth, a defiant expression on her face. The woman ignored it and nodded. "Good. We leave in twenty minutes."

Then she turned and left. The girl beside Cara said, "That is Elettra."

Shaking her head, Cara spat out the pill and asked, "What is with those tits? They look like they belong on some kind of over-sized cow."

The girl laughed, trying to hide her smile behind her hand. "Don't let her hear you say that."

"It's OK. I'll hit her in the chest and deflate her assets."

Another laugh.

"What's your name?"

"Amy."

"Where are you from?"

"South Africa. Cape Town."

"How did you get here?"

Amy hesitated before saying, "They took me from Switzerland. I had stopped over for a few days, and I was drugged in a nightclub."

Cara nodded. It was the same song played on a different banjo. "How long ago was that?"

She shrugged. "A couple of months, I think. I'm not sure. They keep us drugged at different times, so it makes it hard to keep track. I'd better go and get ready."

"Are you going to this thing too?"

"Yes. Unfortunately."

———

"Man, can you believe the set of wheels we have?" Axe almost howled with excitement.

"What were the last words the general said before we left, Axe?" Kane asked him.

"Bring it back in one piece."

"Exactly."

"But you have to admit, man, this thing is fucking hot."

For some reason, one which the Team Reaper commander couldn't understand, Thurston had seen fit to allow them to use an Audi TT RS. A brute of a vehicle, its impressive power capable of hurling it from a standing start to a hundred in a shade under four seconds.

Axe suddenly jammed the brakes on to avoid being T-boned by another vehicle.

"Fuck, Axe. Watch what you're doing," Kane growled.

"Sorry, Reaper. It's what it does to me. This thing is exciting. It was meant to be driven fast."

"Just treat it like you would a woman, Reaper Four," Thurston's voice came over the comms.

"Screw that," Kane snapped. "We'll be upside down in the bushes somewhere."

"Hey, are you saying I don't know how to treat a woman?"

"Hell, Axe. Just forget it. I don't know what I'm saying."

"I do," said Reynolds coming in on the conversation. "I'm sure Mr. Wham-Bam-Thank-You-Ma'am comes from Calgary. Spurs and all."

"Now I am hurt."

"All right, people," Ferrero said, cutting them off. "Concentrate. The target building is around the next corner."

"Hey, Luis," Axe chortled. "Good to hear you back. Have a good holiday?"

"Obviously, it wasn't long enough. Turn left at the next intersection."

At night, Milan was an amazing sight of stunning architecture beautifully lit up, and full of activity; tourists and locals alike. Axe took the turn, the Audi's tires rumbling across steel streetcar tracks. He eased to the curb across from the brothel. A neon sign out front identified it as, *Casa di Piacere*, or House of Pleasure.

Kane said, "Zero, we're outside the target."

"Copy, Reaper One. We have a visual."

The best part about operating in Italy was the Aviano air base. Aviano was providing them with a UAV which would be overhead throughout the mission, even if it was unarmed.

"Reaper One? Bravo Three. We've got your back. The bird gives us a good area of observation. Just don't find any tanks to play with."

"Good to have you back, Master Sergeant."

Kane and Axe climbed from the Audi and started across the cobblestone street, all too aware that they were both unarmed. As they approached the entrance, they saw two burly men standing security on the door. Kane said, "I have two men on the door as security. My bet is that they're armed."

"Copy, Reaper One," acknowledged Ferrero. "Two armed tangos at the front door."

The pair stepped up onto the sidewalk and were about to walk through the door when one of the men blocked their path. He said something in Italian that sounded like a train wreck of words all jumbled together. Axe said, "We're going in there."

The man smiled and nodded. "American. What you want here?"

Axe raised his eyebrows and snapped, "What the fuck you think I want, Mussolini? To stick my dick in your –"

"All right just calm down," Kane intervened. He reached into his pocket and handed over a hundred Euros. "We just want to have a good time."

The security guard took the money and then made a display of opening his coat to reveal the butt of a handgun sticking out of a shoulder holster. "I watch you, American."

Axe smiled. "Please do, you might just learn something."

The man stepped aside, allowing them access to the establishment. Once inside, the first thing Kane noticed was the color of the carpet; red like in a C-grade seventies, porn film. The ornate lamps on the wall were set to dim, and the whole décor bespoke trash. "I thought these things were meant to be high-class?"

"They're called high class for the girls and clientele they attract. But really, a brothel is a brothel," Ferrero said.

"Hey, Reaper, get a look at that."

Kane looked in the direction Axe was pointing and saw the woman behind the counter.

"Is that her?"

Kane nodded. "Zero we have eyes on Elettra Bellandi."

"Copy, Reaper One."

They walked over to the counter, and Elettra looked up from what she was doing. Like the guard, she spoke in Italian. Kane shrugged. "Sorry, we don't speak Italian."

She smiled. "I said, are you a very big man all over?"

Axe chuckled. "They don't call him Horse for nothing, Ma'am."

Elettra's eyes sparkled mischievously. "Really, Mr. Horse. Maybe Elettra could take care of you personally. I like to ride horses."

"Oh, please," Kane heard Thurston say, and could imagine her rolling her eyes.

Kane smiled and couldn't help but say, "That is interesting, Ma'am. I like breaking fillies."

"I'm going to throw up," came through his earpiece.

The former porn starlet thrust out her large breasts and said, "I can assure you that I'm unbreakable."

"Damn it, Reaper," Thurston said through his comms. "Don't encourage her."

Before he could reply to Elettra's obvious challenge, the phone on the desk rang. She scowled, resenting the interruption. Kane glanced at Axe who was openly ogling the woman's half-exposed breasts. He shook his head and heard the tone of Elettra's voice rise. Then her free hand started to wave around angrily, her long nails flashing. She slammed the handset down and snarled, "*Cazzo di stronzo.* I am sorry, *Bambino*, I must attend to something. But I can assure you that all of the girls who work here are most excellent."

Kane made a sorrowful face and said, "That's such a shame. Maybe before I leave Milan, I can come back to visit, yes?"

"Definitely, S*ignore*," Elettra said with a hungry smile. "For now, if you go up the stairs, there will be someone there to meet you."

"Thank you, Ma'am."

"Anytime, Cowboy."

They were about to turn away when an armed man appeared from a back room. He spoke quietly to Elettra who nodded, then followed him out the back.

"Zero, did you get any of that?"

"More than I'd like to, Reaper One."

"The last conversation, Zero."

"Oh, you mean that. Something about an issue with one of the girls at a hotel or some such."

"Copy. We're going upstairs."

They were met on the landing by two young ladies wearing sheer lingerie which would have been their first observation were it not for the guard with a Steyr AUG Bullpup standing in the corner. "He looks friendly," Axe commented.

"Doesn't he just."

The escorts giggled, smiled coyly and took them by the hand. They led them along a hallway furnished with more of the same red carpet as downstairs. Kane took time to note the second guard at the far end. As they passed one of the closed doors, loud moans could be heard from within. They kept on until they reached twin doors side-by-side. Each girl backed into her own room, leading them each by both hands, closing the doors behind them.

CHAPTER 12

Il Magnifico Hotel
Milan

Cara sat in the corner of the ornately-decorated suite and watched as paramedics worked on Addo Chedjou, the Cameroonian ambassador. After everything that she had been through so far, Cara knew that it was bound to happen, but had no idea that when it did, just how violently she would react.

So far, she could work out that the ambassador had a broken jaw, a fractured arm, internal bleeding, and a possible skull fracture from the heavy statue she'd used to hit him with. His bodyguards were both dead.

The man had been a leech, an animal without an appetite for the word no. He'd paid a hefty sum for the woman and meant to get his money's worth.

The evening had started out with dinner at the hotel for any number of African dignitaries from various countries. They had all dined on traditional Italian fare in a large conference hall lavishly decorated with stunning gilding and ornate plaster cornices. Expensive paintings adorned the walls and soft orchestral music played in the background.

The first hint of trouble had come in the form of Chedjou's hand on Cara's thigh below the table. She'd brushed it off forcefully, so there could be no mistaking her response, and the dignitary had turned to look at her. He'd given her a quizzical look and tried again.

Having none of it, Cara had repeated her reaction, more deliberately this time, but bent his finger back until he'd grimaced with pain. "What are you doing?" he'd hissed.

Cara had leaned in close and whispered so only he could hear. "Do it again, and I'll really fucking hurt you."

The confused and galled expression on his face spoke volumes and Cara knew it wouldn't end there. Not by a long sight. She'd finished the rest of her meal and been escorted to the suite upstairs. Once inside the room, Cara was instantly nervous but remained vigilant. One of the bodyguards had come into the suite with them and went to check the other rooms. Cara only had a limited time to prepare, and just as she turned around, Chedjou had hit her a stunning blow up the side of the head.

Cara was staggered but refused to go down. The fire in Chedjou's eyes told her she was in trouble; however, she had been ready for it. As he'd closed on her, she had scooped up a statue and swung it at the dignitary.

Chedjou had held up his right arm to block the blow, and the statue had made heavy contact with it. He'd yelped with pain, drawing the attention of one of his bodyguards. The man had burst into the room and seen what was happening. He'd reached inside his coat to pull his sidearm, but Cara had been too quick. She'd swung the statue again, caving in the side of his head with a sickening thud.

After he'd dropped at her feet, she'd returned her attention to Chedjou. The man had stumbled backward, babbling with fear. Cara, however, was leaving nothing behind. The anger and frustration of recent events boiled over, and the statue once more crashed down in a devastating arc. This time the Cameroonian's jaw broke, although shattered was probably a more appropriate word for it. It rose again then smashed into Chedjou's head. The man dropped like a pole-axed steer and lay there shaking violently.

The door to the room crashed back, and the guard from the hall appeared in the opening. Cara noticed the gun in his hand and immediately dived for the fallen guard's weapon which had spilled free when she'd struck him.

Scooping it up, she brought the weapon into line. God, she hoped it was ready to fire.

BLAM! BLAM! BLAM! BLAM! BLAM! BLAM! BLAM! Then nothing.

The guard lurched violently with each bullet strike, blood flying in a broad spray across walls, the door, and the carpet. The man had dropped to the floor and never moved.

Breathing hard, Cara stared at the three fallen men and sat down. She tossed the empty weapon on the floor and waited for the police to come.

Elettra appeared at the door and walked into the room, accompanied by her personal bodyguard. An Italian *agente di polizia* stepped across to block her progress. She signaled to her bodyguard to fetch Cara while she dealt with the problem.

The bodyguard crossed to Cara who looked up at him with a blank stare. "Get up. We're leaving."

Coming to her feet, she began to walk in front of her escort. As she stepped past Elettra, the woman turned to face her, eyes flaring. "So, you like to hit people? My husband will have just the place for you. Get her in the car."

———

Casa di Piacere
Milan

"You not like me?" the blonde girl asked Kane as she ran a deft hand across his chest, finding his nipple beneath his shirt.

"What's your name?" Kane asked her.

"Kajsa."

"Where are you from?"

"From Sweden."

"Are you here of your own free will?"

Her eyes gave away the lie before she even spoke it. "Of course."

Kane let it slide and then heard the sounds from the room next door and rolled his eyes. "I'm looking for a friend of mine. Are there any new girls?"

"I've seen no one."

"Are you sure? Her name is Cara."

"No."

"Do you know how I can find out?"

Kajsa hesitated, and Kane said, "I can get you out of here."

"No one can do that," the girl's eyes dropped to the floor, full of resignation.

"Let me prove it to you," he said, reaching up to his ear. He took the earbud out and placed it in her ear. "Say hello."

"Hello?"

"Ma'am, my name is Luis Ferrero. Mr. Kane is my man. What he says is true."

Her eyes widened in disbelief, and she took the bud from her ear, looking at it briefly before handing it back. She hesitated before saying, "There is a book. If she is here, her name will be on it."

"Where do they keep it?"

"In the office downstairs."

"OK. Wait here for me."

He exited the room and tried the door to the one next door. It opened, and he found Axe under the covers with the other girl. "Get the hell up. I knew I shouldn't have brought you along."

The ex-recon marine threw back the covers, revealing that he was still fully clothed as was the girl. "We was just getting acquainted."

"We're leaving."

"So soon?"

"Yes. Follow me."

Axe gave the woman a peck on the cheek and said, "See you next time."

Once they were out in the hall, Axe asked, "Where are we going?"

"Downstairs."

He opened the room door where he'd left Kajsa and said, "Come on."

She shook her head. "I can't. You go. Just tell someone about us."

"Reaper, there's a team on the way to get the girls out."

"Roger that," he acknowledged. Then to the girl, he said, "Hang in there. Help is on the way."

"Reaper One, I think you may have a problem."

"What is it, Bravo Three?" Kane asked quietly as they walked along the hall.

"There are three SUVs closing in on your position."

"How the hell did they know we're here?"

"I don't think they do. I think it's Amando Bellandi paying his wife a visit. They'll be with you in two minutes."

"Roger. Zero, permission to go off book?"

"How off book, Reaper One?"

"We may leave a small footprint."

"As long as it is only small, Reaper One, and by small, I am talking minuscule."

Once they were downstairs, Kane had Axe keep an eye out for the guard at the top while he walked over to the counter. This time it was attended by a young red-headed lady who smiled and said, "I hope you enjoyed your experience?"

"Not really," he answered matter-of-factly.

An alarmed expression flitted across her face. "I'm sorry; maybe there is something I can do to help?"

Kane stared at her for a moment and then nodded. "Maybe you can make the experience more pleasurable."

Her face brightened. "Tell me how."

He nodded towards the back room. "How about in there?"

She seemed to hesitate before saying, "Sure."

"Reaper One, inbound tangos one minute out."

They walked through to the back room, which an office of sorts. Kane looked around and saw a row of ledgers on a wall shelf. He hurried across to them and began to pull them down and started flipping through the pages.

"What are you doing?" the girl asked in disbelief.

"I'm trying to find a friend."

"You can't do this."

He glanced at her and saw that she was about to scream. "Wait! Don't scream. Please."

She screamed.

It was a high-pitched, piercing shriek that seemed to echo throughout the building.

"Fuck it," Kane cursed and flicked through the books faster. He found nothing.

Out in the foyer, Axe ducked back behind a pillar when the guard on the landing appeared. The man lumbered down the stairs, and, as soon as he hit the bottom, the big ex-recon marine stepped out and chopped him across the throat, stunning him. The man dropped to his knees, and Axe kicked him in the face. Axe then picked up the Steyr and waited for the other man to appear.

"Reaper, you need to get your fucking ass out of there now."

"Give me a minute," Kane said as he tossed the last book aside. He looked over at the frozen girl and said, "Where is the ledger?"

"Wh – what?"

"The book Elettra uses for the girls. Where is it?"

Her eyes flicked towards the desk, and she said, "I don't know."

"Thanks," Kane said and walked over to it. He slid open the top drawer and found what he was looking for.

"Reaper One, the tangos are pulling up now."

"Copy."

A loud burst of automatic fire ripped through the brothel, and Axe shouted, "Reaper, we gotta go!"

Kane looked at the girl. "Is there a back way out?"

"There," she said, pointing to another door.

"Axe, come this way."

More gunfire erupted, and Axe said, "Be right there, Reaper."

Another burst of fire was followed by an anguished cry and the sound of someone falling down the stairs. Axe appeared in the doorway and smiled. "I'm right to go now."

Kane held up the ledger. "Got it. We're going out the back."

Axe gave the redhead his most endearing smile, and they hurried out through the door and into a wide alley. It was dark outside, but the light from the open door spilled onto the street enough to show the way. "We'll circle back to the car. Bravo Three, how are we looking?"

"The tangos have gone inside. You need to move."

Axe dumped the Steyr as they jogged along the alley and circled back around the block, walking towards their Audi on the opposite side of the street. Out front of the brothel, four men had emerged and appeared to be looking around for them.

One of the men looked up and eyeballed Kane. He shouted something and pointed across the street. "Get in, Axe. We've been rumbled."

They jumped into the Audi just as the men across the street opened fire with their weapons. The bullets striking the panels sounded like a hail storm, and the side window shattered, spraying the pair with glass just as Axe got the engine to fire.

He wrenched the stick into gear and floored the accelerator. The wheels spun, and the Audi fishtailed out into the traffic, almost collecting an oncoming vehicle.

"Christ!" Kane exclaimed. "That went well."

Axe was looking in the rearview mirror and said grimly, "We aren't done yet. They've decided they still want the pleasure of our company."

Kane cast a glance back over his shoulder and saw that an SUV had peeled out and was now following. "Bravo Three, we have company. I need a way out of here."

"Copy, Reaper One. I'm on it."

"Axe, turn left here," Kane snapped.

The ex-recon man hit the brakes and spun the wheel left. The rear end slid around the corner, forcing the driver to correct before it kept going. Axe floored the throttle once more, and the Audi shot forward.

"Reaper One, at the next intersection, you need to turn left."

"Copy, Bravo Three." Kane gripped the handle on the door as the vehicle accelerated.

Behind them, headlights bounced into view, their beams reflecting from the rearview mirror. "Axe, you need to turn left at the next intersection."

There was no response as the Audi lurched over a bump in the cobblestones and almost became airborne. The turn was coming on at a speed which seemed impossible for the Audi to make safely. At the last possible moment, Axe jammed on the brakes, spun the wheel, and turned ...

... right!

"Left!" Kane shouted. "Left! Left! You were told to turn fucking left!"

Axe said nothing as he began dodging the oncoming traffic.

"Reaper One, you've just turned the wrong way onto a one-way street."

"No shit, Bravo Three. Axe, turn this bitch around!"

Axe swerved around a car whose horn blared loudly and then pulled on the parking brake while turning hard on the wheel. The car's rear end whipped around and straightened, now going with the flow of traffic.

Headlights from the pursuing SUV lit them up in its beams, dazzling both men. Suddenly muzzle flashes from the oncoming vehicle winked at them, an indication that the passenger had just opened fire. Kane accessed the glove compartment where he'd left his M17. He pressed the button to lower the window then put his arm out the opening to fire when suddenly Axe slid the Audi into a ninety-degree turn to the right.

"What the hell are you doing?" Kane barked above the squeal of tires.

"Hang on!" he exclaimed, and the vehicle's nose dropped as it began a sharp descent down a wide set of stairs.

The Audi bucked wildly, and Kane heard Teller in his comms say, "That'll work."

When they reached the bottom, a wide piazza opened before them. Axe put his foot down to accelerate across the cobbled expanse. Behind them, Kane saw the SUV finish its careening run down the steps and follow.

"Reaper One, across the other side of the piazza there is a street. Once you reach it, turn right."

"Copy, Bravo Three."

"And watch out for the –"

"Oh, fuck!" Axe exclaimed as a large marble fountain loomed up in front of them. He wrenched the wheel to the left, and the Audi responded immediately. The rear end kicked out, just missing the fountain's raised pond, which could have done serious damage to the vehicle.

"I guess you found the fountain, Reaper One?"

"More like it nearly found us."

Axe turned the wheel the other way and put them back on track. Behind them, there were now two SUVs in pursuit. The one in front was closer since their near miss had cost them precious time, and the passenger opened fire again.

Bullets peppered the back of the Audi, and the rear window was shattered by a couple of rounds. Axe snapped, "Are you going to shoot back or what?"

"Just drive. When you hit the street on the other side of the piazza, turn left."

"Why left?"

"Because I'm hoping you'll turn fucking right."

"Why didn't you just say right?"

"Because you don't listen."

Axe twisted the wheel suddenly to avoid a couple walking across in front of them. "I listen. I'm a good listener."

"What way are you going to turn, Axe?"

"Left."

Kane shook his head. "Fuck me. Stop the car!"

"What?"

"Stop the damned car!"

Axe jammed on the brakes, and the Audi slid to a halt. Kane leaped from the vehicle, walked behind it and raised the M17. He blasted ten rounds from the seventeen-round magazine at the lead SUV which took a violent turn to the right and rolled. Pieces of shattered glass flew in all directions, and behind it, the second SUV had to veer hard left to avoid a collision, roaring past the inert Audi.

Kane nonchalantly continued to the driver's door and yanked it open. "Get over."

"Damn it, Reaper ..."

"Now, Axe."

The ex-recon marine climbed into the passenger seat which Kane had just vacated. He looked through the windshield and saw the second SUV turn abruptly and start coming back towards them. "You might want to hurry up, Reaper, before these guys start shooting."

Kane climbed into the Audi and tossed Axe his M17. "Here, shoot the fuckers back."

Without another word, Kane put it into gear and planted his foot. The tires squealed, and the Audi shot forward.

Axe leaned out the window and fired four shots at the oncoming SUV, which were returned in spades when the shooter inside it let loose with a Steyr.

"Reaper One, we're getting traffic over the net telling us that you have police converging on your position. Suggest you turn left instead of right once you leave the piazza."

"Shit!" Kane cursed.

The SUV slid past them on the right leaving an open run to the street ahead. Luckily there were no more pedestrians, which made navigation easier.

However, another problem soon arose. Dirty great steel bollards had been erected along the edge of the piazza, a sign of the times and designed to stop anyone who might have a notion to use their car as a weapon.

"Damn it!" Kane cursed out loud, putting the vehicle into a sliding turn. "Slick, are you there?"

"Copy, Reaper One."

"We need some of your magic. We've got bollards

blocking our exfil. They look electric; can you do something with them?"

"I'll try."

The pursuing SUV shifted track when its driver saw the Audi coming back their way, pointing the vehicle's nose at them and attempting to pin the side panel. Kane's quick acceleration managed to avoid the potentially-crippling blow.

He circled back around the fountain and pointed the Audi towards the bollards. "Slick, I need those things down now."

"Just about there, Reaper."

Axe leaned out the window and fired back at the SUV. One of its headlights went out suddenly, smashed by a lucky shot. The armed passenger lit them up with a long burst, and more holes opened in the Audi.

"Come on, Slick. We're about to run out of car."

"Right now, Reaper. Go now."

Kane floored the accelerator and the vehicle's rear end kicked out a touch before its tires gained traction as it straightened, shooting forward with an amazing burst of speed. Axe fired more shots out the rear window, and the SUV dropped back.

Kane's eyes widened with the sudden realization that the bollards, although retracting slowly, were not going to be down by the time they got there. He dropped the Audi back a gear and punched the throttle, swinging on the wheel once more. Axe's head snapped around. "Damn it, Reaper, what are you ... whoa!"

"Hang on, Axe!"

The ex-recon marine gripped the seat beside him as the rear end of the Audi kicked out once more. Kane punched the accelerator again and pointed it back the way they'd come.

"You get the feeling we're going around in circles, Reaper?"

"You think?"

"What's wrong, Reaper One?"

"The damned bollards aren't down. They're going too slow."

The shooter from the SUV fired again, and Kane swerved the vehicle to make less of a target. "Do something about him, will you? I thought you were supposed to be some hotshot sniper."

Axe slapped a fresh magazine home into the SIG. "If you weren't driving around like a drunken maniac, I'd be right."

"Here then, try this."

Kane jammed on the brakes and turned the wheel. The Audi slid sideways, presenting the SUV as a clear target. Axe poked the M17 through the opening, blowing off half of the seventeen-shot magazine.

The rounds impacted the windscreen and hit the driver. The SUV lurched left, and the tires bit, throwing the vehicle over and over. Kane and Axe watched as it tumbled past the front of the Audi and Kane nodded with satisfaction. "About time."

"Reaper One, you've got police converging on your position from multiple directions. I suggest you get out of there."

"Copy, Bravo Three. See you when we get home."

———

Team Reaper Ops Center
Milan, Italy

. . .

On the outskirts of Milan, the team was holed up in a warehouse utilized by the CIA during operations into Bosnia, Croatia, and Serbia. Externally, it looked disused, seeming to be in a terrible state of disrepair; however, the inside told a much different story.

When Kane and Axe drew up in the Audi, they were met by Traynor who took one look at the car and shook his head. "Mama ain't going to be happy with her boys tonight."

"Shut up," Kane growled. "If Axe could drive, we'd have had no problem."

"That would be right, blame the subordinate," Axe protested. "Besides, it ain't that bad."

Traynor chuckled. "No, you're right; it's worse."

Then the inevitable happened. Thurston appeared at the door and stopped as though she'd been shot. She glared at the men before her, who pointed at each other and said simultaneously, "He did it."

"Unbelievable. Eighty-five thousand dollars' worth of car and you two fuck it up in one evening. I knew I should have got you a damned pickup."

"In all fairness, Ma'am, it wasn't exactly us who shot it up."

"I don't want to hear it. The general will have heart failure when he gets the bill for this. Inside. Briefing in five minutes."

They watched her go, and Kane turned to his friend. "All because you couldn't follow a simple direction."

"Yes, sir. Mama definitely ain't happy with her boys tonight," Traynor chuckled once more.

They both turned to him and said, "Shut up."

Once inside, Kane handed the ledger over to Swift who

took it across to his work station and started going through it. Ferrero turned and saw Kane and opened his mouth to speak.

"Before you say anything, the general has already torn strips off us."

"I was just going to say that it's good to see you in one piece."

"Thanks."

"Did you find out anything?"

"Apart from the fact that these guys are well armed? Not really."

"While you were on your way back, we picked up something through other channels."

"What?"

"Wait for the briefing."

"OK."

They gathered around, and Thurston signaled Swift to join them. He grabbed his coffee cup and crossed to them with the ledger under his arm. He took a seat with the others and waited for the general to begin.

With a lengthy sigh, she said, "I wouldn't exactly call that a successful mission, people. However, Interpol has raided the club and taken the girls there into custody. There was no sign of Bellandi or his wife."

"What about the ledger? Surely there is something in that?" Kane asked.

"There are a few interesting bits in there," Swift said, standing up. "I haven't had time to look at it in depth. There are some new girls, but their names are coded. There are a few notes beside them, one of which stands out. There was a dinner at the Il Magnifico Hotel. There were marks next to the names of certain code names which indicate that some of the girls were going there."

"That doesn't tell us much," Axe said. "Just that there was a dinner at the hotel, and some girls were going there."

"It tells us more than you know," Thurston said. "Slick, continue."

"There was some trouble at the hotel earlier this evening. Apparently, a dignitary from Cameroon was badly beaten, and his two bodyguards were shot and killed. By a woman."

Kane nodded. "That sounds like our woman. So, the police will have her?"

"That's what we thought, but they don't. She was taken away by a woman and a man. All accounts say that it was Elettra and her bodyguard."

"So, we're back to square one," Kane pointed out. "We have no idea what has happened to her or even if she is still alive."

"That's about it."

Kane shook his head. "What a fuck up."

"My thoughts exactly."

CHAPTER 13

Turin, Italy

Kane and Arenas made their way through the cheering crowd as two women in a cage virtually beat the shit out of each other. After two weeks, the search for information had finally borne fruit, even if it was only half-grown.

According to several sources, Amando Bellandi had a fight setup in Turin. It was exclusively women's MMA (mixed martial arts). Apparently, Bellandi had a new fighter who was taking all who came before her. Upon hearing the news, Thurston had dispatched Kane and Arenas to investigate, in the hope that it would draw a satisfactory conclusion.

"Zero, we're in."

"Copy, Reaper One."

Inside the cage, a well-muscled woman with red hair let loose with a roundhouse kick that caught her brunette opponent under the jaw. The dark-haired woman's head snapped back, and she buckled at the knees before falling to the canvas. The red-head danced around the cage with her hands raised, cheering.

Two men entered the ring and dragged the unconscious fighter out while the remaining woman played up to the boisterous crowd.

Arenas nudged Kane and indicated a man seated ring-side with a familiar woman. "Zero, I have eyes on Amando and Elettra Bellandi."

"Copy. Watch your backs."

The pair began to circle the ring, trying to locate the change rooms. Before they got too far, things began to happen. Firstly, a new fighter appeared, emerging from an unseen place, likely the change rooms they sought. A tall, raven-haired woman with thick arms and a muscular physique. The second thing was more personal. Cara mate-rialized from the cheering crowd, dressed in a white crop top and tight-fitting Spandex shorts. Her fists were taped, and she looked to be in peak physical condition.

Kane said, "Zero, I've spotted the package. I'm moving to intercept."

"Copy, Reaper One."

Kane and Arenas reached behind their backs to draw their M17s when Thurston's voice flashed over the net. "Stand down, Reaper One. I say again, Stand down."

"Repeat, please, Bravo. Did you say stand down?"

"Affirmative. Wait my next."

Kane glanced at Arenas and saw a similar confused expression on his face to what was on his own. What the hell was happening?

AISE Safehouse

Turin, Italy

"Stop this operation now!" *Agenzia Informazioni e Sicurezza Esterna* agent Efisio Capello demanded as he burst into the room, flanked by two other agents from Italian intelligence.

Thurston whirled around, staring at the man with slicked-back hair and beady eyes, a look of irritation on her face. "What do you mean stop? Your people signed off on this operation to get our person back."

"That was before they knew it was Bellandi who had her."

"Stand down, Reaper One. I say again, stand down."

A pause.

"Affirmative. Wait my next."

"Good," Capello said with a curt nod. "Now, you will recall your men."

"The hell I will."

"If you do not, I will have you out of this country within the hour."

Thurston's face was clouded with rage. Through gritted teeth, she asked, "Why? Tell me why I should leave my person in the hands of this killer?"

"We are currently in the middle of an investigation of Bellandi's whole operation. If you do this, it will jeopardize many months of hard work."

A million thoughts raced through the general's mind until one stuck. "What if we could help you with him? Take the son of a bitch off the map."

"How?"

"He imports drugs, right?"

"Yes."

"Drugs are what we are good at. What if we could stop him and get our person back at the same time?"

"Keep talking."

"I take it that you have the locations of his operations."

"Yes."

"How about we have our people raid one of those locations, confiscate whatever we find, and then set up a trade for our person? Then you and your team can be on hand to take him down once we have her back."

Capello looked skeptical but nodded his agreement. "OK. But if this goes wrong, you and your people are out of Italy for good."

"It won't go wrong," Thurston said. Then, "Reaper One, abort mission."

"Say again?"

"You heard me. Mission terminated. RTB."

———

Turin, **_Italy_**

Kane was incredulous. The words he was hearing were almost incomprehensible. He was being ordered to leave a teammate behind for a second time. When it happened the first time, it went against everything he stood for. This time it was unforgivable.

"Ma'am ..." he started to protest but was cut off by Ferrero.

"Reaper One, follow the damned order. Abort the fucking mission."

"Yes, sir."

The two men started towards the door, anger coursing

through their veins. When Kane looked back one last time, Cara had just stepped into the cage. "Hang in there, Cara. We'll get you back home."

———

Cara flexed her aching muscles and brought up her taped fists. Her third fight in a week, and it was beginning to tell on her body, both visually and internally. She was almost certain she carried a busted rib from her last fight as well as the bruises on her face and body. Her facial ones, however, weren't as bad at the others.

The upside of it was that at least now she had a way of releasing her pent-up rage, and no one was trying to rape her.

Her first fight had lasted all of one minute. She was sure that it had been a test to see how good she was. The second was against a much stronger opponent, and she'd taken some serious blows before working out the woman's weakness and exploiting it.

This one, however, was different. Cara had heard talk in the back room that Bellandi had picked the woman especially for this fight and bet heavily upon her. Apparently, she was ex-Italian military, and Bellandi stood to win a lot of money if she could defeat the American.

Which meant that Cara would have to beat her quickly if she was to have a chance. The longer the fight went on, the less likely that she would come out on top. Who knew what sort of serious injuries she might sustain, maybe even a fatal one.

The worst part was that there were no breaks, no rounds. It was fight until the victor was the only one left standing.

The opponent exuded aggression and came at Cara with a confidence designed to put her on the back foot from the outset. So, she let her come, and when a flying right elbow came at Cara, designed to finish it quickly, Cara dropped to her knees, ducked under the elbow, and hit the woman a solid blow to her middle, stopping her in her tracks.

Gasping for air, the woman stepped back. Cara leaped to her feet and hit her in the face with a clenched fist. Blood spurted onto the canvas floor in large droplets from a broken nose. Cara hit her again, this time with a right elbow that almost shattered the woman's jaw.

Every blow was telling, but the last was devastating. The woman's eyes took on a glazed appearance as the lights slowly began to fade and unconsciousness set in. Another blow was totally unnecessary, but Cara wanted to make a point to Bellandi, who sat in his seat, stunned at the outcome.

Around him, the crowd went into raptures at the overwhelmingly powerful performance they were witnessing. Cara stared at him, making sure he made eye contact with her before she spat on the canvas and whirled about, bringing up her right foot in a powerful roundhouse kick.

The Italian woman's jaw broke under the impact as she was spun around by the force and crashed to the canvas, out cold. Cara had defeated her without so much as getting a hand laid on her person.

The angry glare on Bellandi's face said it all. He was far from happy that his scheme had failed. Rising from his seat, he pushed his way through the crowd, his wife and bodyguard following him.

CHAPTER 14

Team Reaper Briefing
Milan, Italy

This is where Bellandi stores a sizable portion of his drugs,"
Capello explained, showing the team a large satellite
picture exposure. "It is a furniture factory outside of
Milan."

Kane studied the photo and asked, "Where do they
keep the drugs?"

The AISE agent sighed. "We're not sure. We know they
are there, but the exact location is uncertain."

He brought up a blueprint of the factory and indicated
an area towards the rear. "We think that the drugs are there.
However, according to our sources, there is a basement
underneath the factory, which is another possibility."

"Why can't your source confirm the location if he can
tell you that there is a basement?" Axe asked.

"Our source is one of the men who constructed it many

years ago. We cannot get anyone on the inside to speak because they are all scared of Bellandi."

"Any security cameras that are accessible?" Kane asked.

"No."

"So, we're going in blind?" Axe asked.

"I'm sorry, but we thought this was the best one for your team to hit. It is the furthest away, which means that it will take the longest time for reinforcements to travel to the site."

Kane stared at Capello. "What reinforcements?"

"Bellandi can have twenty men there within fifteen minutes once the alarm is raised."

"Then we'll have to go in quietly. How many men does he have on site?"

"Ten at any one time. They are all well trained."

"Why haven't your people taken this *hombre* off the map?" Arenas asked.

"Because he is like the octopus. He has tentacles everywhere. Whenever we try to arrest him, he is forewarned, and we get nothing."

"So, what is different this time?" Ferrero asked.

"I have told no one."

"Isn't that kind of dangerous for you?" Kane commented.

"Only if you get caught," Capello said with a nod. "But I must ask one thing of you. If you succeed, and you are able to set up the trade, I would like for you to kill Bellandi."

Kane's head snapped up. "I thought you were taking him in alive?"

Capello shook his head. "We cannot. If he goes before a judge, he is as good as free."

"So, you want us to kill him for you?"

"Yes."

Axe smiled as he said, "I think we can accommodate you there."

Kane looked at Thurston and Ferrero. "This is your call. I don't like being someone else's hitman, but this guy needs to be taken off the board."

They both nodded. Thurston said, "Do it."

"Can we have a UAV over the target area with thermal imaging?" Kane asked.

Everyone looked towards Reynolds and Teller. The former said, "Sure, if we're allowed to fly it in Italian airspace?"

Capello snorted. "Please, I already know that you have had one operational at least once since you have been here."

"I'll take that as a yes."

"Thermals will help," Teller allowed. "At least you won't be blind. But instead of an MQ-9 Reaper, why don't we try for something a little smaller?"

"What did you have in mind?"

"A Wasp III, nice and compact, will do the job."

"Don't you have to be close with that one?"

"One of the team could fly it."

"There's no time to teach them," Kane said. "Brooke, can you do it?"

"Sure."

"Good, break out your kit, you'll be coming with us. You and Traynor can sit outside the perimeter while we breach."

Teller said, "The Wasp can be programmed to fly autonomously."

Kane shook his head. "I want someone in control of that thing at all times. It's a good idea though. We'll insert tomorrow night. Full combat gear. We neutralize all threats before we even move on the target. The key is to be able to get in without the alarm being raised."

Arenas turned his gaze to Capello. "Can we expect any help from your people?"

"No. You are not even here. According to my superiors, you flew out earlier today."

"How is it your people are scared of this man?"

"He operates like the Mexican Cartels. This man even scares the Mafia."

"Well, once we're done, no one will fear him again," Thurston pointed out.

"I hope you are right."

―――――

Team Reaper
Milan, Italy

"Reaper One? Bravo One. The Wasp is in the air."

"Copy, Bravo One."

The Wasp III was a UAS, Unmanned Aerial System, which was classed as a micro-system. It was mainly used for surveillance and recon in combat situations and could operate at low altitude. It was compact and could fit into a briefcase when broken down and was only armed with a high-resolution day/night camera. But for what the team was about to do, it was ideal.

A few minutes after being hand launched, Reynolds came back over the comms. "Reaper One, I have visual, over."

"Copy, Bravo One. We're moving."

Blocking their path was a chain-link perimeter fence. Axe set about cutting an access hole while Arenas pulled rear security. After a couple of minutes, the hole was big enough for them to pass through. "Reaper Team entering target."

"Reaper One? Bravo One. You have two tangos headed your way from your two o'clock. Three more are patrolling various parts of the perimeter, and another five are inside the factory. Three are on the ground level while two more are on the first floor."

"Roger."

Kane moved through the opening first and waited on the other side while the others followed. Each man wore a ballistic vest with ammo pouches full. Helmets carried NVGs which were dropped into place, and all three carried suppressed HK416s with laser sights.

"Reaper One, you should have visual on your tangos any moment."

"Copy."

Kane waited on a knee, Arenas beside him, for the two perimeter guards. When they appeared, they were walking side-by-side, oblivious to the team's presence. Once they were within range, both operatives raised their weapons; the lasers reaching out like lances onto the guards' chests. Two shots apiece were fired, dropping the men like stones down a well.

"This is Reaper One. We're moving to secure the perimeter."

With virtually no noise, the three operators started to circle the factory. Outside the perimeter, Reynolds worked the Wasp tracking their movements and those of Bellandi's security. "Reaper One, you have a third guard at your twelve o'clock."

As she watched the screen, she saw the red and orange glow of the figure fall to the ground. Then Kane's voice came over the comms, "Tango down."

"Reaper One, you've two more around the far side of the factory. It looks like they've stopped for a chat."

"Copy, Bravo One."

"Reaper," said Axe. "I'll take care of them. You head inside and clean them out of there."

"All right. Watch your ass."

Axe moved swiftly towards the corner of the building, while Kane and Arenas located the door they were meant to breach. The Mexican reached out and tried the door. It opened without resistance. Both men lifted their NVGs, and Arenas pushed the door open wide enough for Kane to enter and sweep the other side of the opening.

"Bravo One, call it."

"Roger that. You have a tango to your right, behind what appears to be a stack of crates."

Kane and Arenas moved swiftly, and the guard was surprised when two armed men appeared in front of him. Kane put him down with two shots, and then they moved on to the next target. Within minutes, the ground floor was clear, with two more going down without any hassles, and they moved to the first floor, achieving a similar outcome.

Kane said into his mic, "Reaper Four, sitrep?"

"Two tangos down outside, Reaper."

"Inside is clear too. Come on in."

They worked their way through to the back of the factory where they found the entrance to the basement. Moving silently down the stairs on rubber-soled boots, they then entered a dark room. Using his NVGs, Kane located a switch for the lights and turned it on. The trio flicked up their night vision as the lights came up, then inhaled deeply at the sight that lay before them.

"Zero, we have a bit of a situation here."

"Copy, Reaper. What seems to be the problem?"

"We've found no drugs, only some money."

"Roger that. How much money, Reaper One?"

"I'm not really sure."

"OK, take a wild guess."

"I'd say at least two-hundred million. We're going to need a truck."

———

Milan, Italy

The grand total of what Bellandi had stored in the basement was actually two-hundred and sixty million. But not anymore. Within an hour, it had been cleared out and transported to a safe location. Now, just after ten the following morning, the team were gathered around throwing ideas back and forth working out their next move.

"We set up a meeting with Bellandi, isn't it obvious?" Axe asked.

Capello shook his head. "Not if he doesn't want to be found."

"What about his wife?" asked Kane. "Do we know where she is?"

Swift filled in the blank. "Her and Bellandi have a large house, one of many, outside of Milan. I've tracked her there."

"Is she on her own?"

"As far as I can tell, there are five guards watching over her."

"Give me an address, and I'll pay her a visit."

Thurston asked, "Are you sure you want to go on your own?"

"I'm a big boy."

"OK, but stay on comms."

"Sure."

Kane went to the bathroom and tidied himself up, making sure that he looked his best, then got the address from Swift and took one of the team's SUVs. As he drove across Milan towards his target, his mind wandered to Cara and what she must be going through. It didn't take long before the GPS navigator announced that he had arrived at his destination, the Bellandi house. Except it wasn't a house, it was a mansion. Driving up to a pair of ornate wrought iron gates, he reached his arm out the window and pressed the button.

"Si?"

"It's your friendly neighborhood horse."

There was a moment of silence, and then the gates began to swing open. When there was enough space to admit his vehicle, Kane drove through and up to the front steps of the impressive house. He was met there by Elettra and two of her bodyguards. While the men were attired formally in suits and ties, the former porn starlet had dressed down for the occasion and had on a too-small bikini top and a micro mini skirt with more tanned skin on display than was covered.

Kane climbed out and shut the door on the SUV. He made a show of looking around at the double-story façade and said, "Quite a place you have here."

"You are either very brave or very stupid, Mister Horse. Which is it?"

He smiled, remembering the name. "My friends call me Reaper."

"I do not think that we are friends."

"That's a shame. It wasn't that long ago you wanted to

be more than friends," he said, smiling and raising his eyebrows at her.

"That would have been a mistake."

"I guess we'll never know. Are you going to invite me in?" He indicated the house with an expansive gesture.

"Why should I? One word and my men will kill you."

"I want to talk business with your husband," Kane explained.

"He's not here. He has had an emergency."

"But you are. Perhaps you could pass it on."

Elettra thought for a moment and said, "Follow me."

Kane smiled. "With pleasure."

When he reached the top of the tiled steps, one of the bodyguards moved to block his path. Kane reached around behind himself and took out the M17. He handed it over, and Elettra said, "That's a big gun, Reaper."

"Not as big as some that I have."

"We'll see."

He followed her through the lavish home and out through a set of open bi-fold door panels into a lush garden area beside a sparkling inground pool. There were another two guards dressed the same as the others; however, these were armed with Steyrs.

Elettra sat on a large outdoor lounge on one side of a glass table. Kane sat opposite her on a matching one. Almost immediately, a slim, well-dressed maid appeared with several glasses of wine. His host took a glass, her long polished nails sparkling around the delicate stem. She looked at him and asked, "Would you like a drink?"

Kane shook his head. "I don't drink while I'm working."

She shrugged. "Have it your way."

Elettra brought the receptacle seductively up to her luscious lips, prolonging the moment of sipping as though she was drinking the nectar of the gods. When she leaned forward to place it back on the table, Kane's eyes were instantly drawn towards her heavy breasts, barely restrained by the minuscule bikini top.

She leaned back and asked, "What is it you wish to discuss?"

"You have a friend of mine working for you. The last I saw of her, she was about to fight in one of your cage matches."

"It is a woman?" Elettra asked, raising her finely-plucked eyebrows.

Kane nodded, making eye contact to see her reaction.

Studying him for a moment, she slowly began putting things together in her mind. Then, "She is the one they call Cara, yes?"

"That's her."

"She is a very good fighter. Why should we let her go?"

"I was hoping we could come to some kind of arrangement."

Elettra rose from her seat and walked around the table. She sat next to Kane, crossed her legs, and placed her hand on his thigh. "Shall we discuss your arrangement?"

Leaning in close, she kissed him on the lips. He eased her back gently with both hands and looked around at the guards. "Do not worry about them; they see nothing."

She picked up his right hand and placed it on her breast. Beneath the flimsy fabric, he felt her nipple harden. "Is that better?"

"I was kind of hoping for some other arrangement."

She sat back and pouted. "It seems that you are going to great lengths not to spend some time with me. It is not something I'm willing to get used to."

"If you remember, we're not exactly friends," Kane pointed out.

"We don't have to be friends to fuck," Elettra retorted.

"No, I guess you're right there."

She sighed. "What could you possibly have that would be worth such a sum for my husband to let go a prized possession?"

"How about two-hundred and sixty million Euros?"

The seductive smile was immediately wiped from her face, and the guards moved closer as they sensed the change in her demeanor. One of them took another step forward, and she held up a slender-fingered hand. "No, it is OK."

Kane said, "You look a little pale. Perhaps you should have another drink?"

"You bastard pig!" she spat vehemently.

"I guess sex is out of the question now, huh?"

Elettra rattled off a string of invective in Italian, which Kane didn't understand but caught the gist by the tone used. In his ear, a voice said, "Missed out again; Reaper. I'd have done it the other way around."

Frigging Axe.

"All I want is a meeting with your husband, and we can make a trade. My friend for the money."

She stared at him with angry eyes. "I will have to talk to him."

Kane reached into his pocket and took out a piece of paper with a cell number on it. "This is where he can reach me."

He looked up while she glanced down at the number then looked back at him once again. Elettra said, "My husband is not a forgiving man. I suggest you find a rock to climb under and never come out. If you do, he will cut your fucking head off."

"I'll be waiting for his call."

Kane stood up and walked over to the guard who had taken his M17 earlier. He held out his hand for the weapon, but the man hesitated, flicking his eyes over Kane's shoulder, giving away what was to come.

Kane's training kicked in, and he moved with swift precision. His right hand reached in under the guard's coat, coming out with a Beretta, while his left grabbed the man's right arm, dragging it up behind his back and pulling him close. The guard was slow to respond and paid the price for his laxity with pain from his twisted shoulder. Kane brought the Beretta up and aimed center mass at the closest guard.

Two shots thundered, and the guard fell with two holes in his chest. Kane shifted aim and put two rounds into one of the guards with the Steyr. The other guard with the same weapon rattled off a couple of careless rounds which hammered into the man Kane was using to shield himself. Each bullet jolted the guard, and Kane felt the impacts through the body in his hands.

The Team Reaper leader aimed at the remaining shooter and put a slug into the center of his face. Nothing like a bullet right there to slow you down; permanently.

He let go of the wounded man who slid to the clay pavers at his feet. Before bending down to retrieve his M17, he glanced at Elettra. Her face was pale with shock at the sudden violence. Kane dropped the Beretta on the ground and waited, M17 in his hand. The fifth guard appeared through the rear glass doors, handgun raised. Two bullets from the M17 put him down without any hassles.

Kane said to Elettra, "I was going to leave here nice and quiet. Their deaths are on you."

"Get out!" she screeched. *"Get out! Get out! Get out!"*

———

Milan, Italy

The door opened, and Amando Bellandi walked through the opening, flanked by Carlo Laurito and one of his other bodyguards. He stared at her and said, "Get up."

Slowly Cara came to her feet. "Am I fighting again?"

"No. You are leaving. It would appear you are more trouble than you are worth."

"Where am I going?"

"Vatican City."

"Why not just kill me?"

"Because you are worth a great deal of money to me. I'm sure the Brothers will find a use for you once you arrive."

Cara's blood ran cold. There was a look in Bellandi's eyes that troubled her. "Who are the Brothers?"

"Priests. Carlo will take you to them."

"Why would priests want me?"

"They're not exactly priests; they're druids. And it is not just you. There will be other girls with you."

"Druids?"

"Yes, druids."

———

Milan, Italy

At noon, the day after Kane's visit to Elettra Bellandi, the cell in Kane's pocket buzzed, and he retrieved it, looking over to Ferrero who asked, "What is it?"

"I think it's him."

"Put it on speaker."

Kane did so. "Hello?"

"Is this Reaper?"

"It is."

"I understand that you were at one of my many homes yesterday?"

"That's right. Are you Bellandi?"

"Yes. I believe you wish to make a trade?"

"That's right. Your money for my friend."

"Fine."

The response was too quick by far, and Kane glanced up at Ferrero who pulled a face. Kane shrugged and said, "How do you want to do this?"

"There is a small village in the Apennines, called Bucolic where I have a house. We will do the trade there."

"How will I know it?"

"You will work it out. You have two days. Come alone."

"Not going to happen. You will have men, and so will I."

"One extra, then. If I see any more than that, I will kill the woman. Oh, and tell Agent Capello, I said hello."

The line went dead, and Kane looked from the phone to Ferrero and said, "That was too easy."

Ferrero nodded his assent. "All except for the fact he knows that Capello is involved. Yes, way too easy. He's up to something."

"We need to find out all we can about this place before we go in there."

"Capello will know."

When they found the intelligence man, he was talking to Thurston, and they explained about the call and the proposed meeting. Capello looked concerned. "I know of the place he is talking about, and there is a good reason he picked it."

"Which is?" Kane prompted.

"He owns the town. It is in the Apennines Mountains. It was once a ghost town? Yes, I think that is correct. The valley that it is situated in is only accessible through a pass. So, once you are in there, he has you trapped. If you go in there, you will not come out."

Kane nodded. "It's not a case of going in; it's how we go in."

"He will have a lot of men waiting for you."

"He'll have less when we leave," Kane told him. "Can you get maps and aerial photographs?"

"*Si.*"

"Great. Luis, I'm going to need one more thing."

"I'll see what I can do."

"It worries me that he knows so much. I'll take Axe with me and leave Arenas here as a backup gun. Besides, I figure they'll know if I take anyone else with me."

"You figure he'll try to hit us here?"

"We took his money, so yeah, maybe he's a little pissed. But what I want from you is this ..."

Kane went on to tell him of his plan. When he was finished, Ferrero nodded and said, "I'll have to run it past the general, but I think it could work. But we still only have a couple of days to put it together."

"I guess we'd better get right to it then."

CHAPTER 15

Sangin Valley, Afghanistan

An aerial view of the area surrounding the Sangin River showed a mass of green. It might seem as though someone had taken a Crayon and drawn some lines then colored between those borders green. That's what that part of the country was like. A short distance away, however, the green stopped suddenly, and the image became brown and arid.

The scenery aside, Bluey and his boys weren't there for the view. Theirs was an important capture or kill mission. Two days before, a small force of Afghan troops, along with their US advisors had been ambushed while patrolling the river area. Out of a force of twenty, eleven were killed, including two of the three Americans.

Word had come down from intelligence that the leader of the Taliban responsible was Diliwar Jahan, an insurgent who had coordinated many attacks throughout the Sangin area. Chatter placed him at a compound owned by his brother-in-law, and HQ wanted him gone.

Five kilometers to the north of the SAS team's current position, gunfire rattled out followed by the CRUMP of something heavier, probably a mortar. It was there that a company of ANA troops, accompanied by a squad of advisors had started a patrol to draw the Taliban out towards them with the sole purpose of engagement. The ensuing battle was meant to keep the insurgents away from where Bluey and his team were. As for Jahan, headquarters was hoping that he would hunker down in place, unwilling to poke his head above ground so soon again. So far, ICOM chatter seemed to support that theory.

Each SAS man was armed with a suppressed M4A5, except for Lofty who carried the HK417. No use in attracting unwanted attention if they could get away with it. They moved forward silently, cautiously, under cover of thick trees before they came upon some open, tilled ground.

Jacko was on point, and he dropped to his knee, M4 still up to his shoulder, covering the area before him. Bluey settled in beside him and waited for him to speak.

"I don't like it, Bluey. There's a lot of open ground between us and our target over there," he said, pointing at the mud wall on the other side of the compound. "If they're alerted, they'll have someone watching, and it'll get nasty."

Behind them, the rest of the team took up security positions while the two men discussed their next moves. Bluey said, "There's an irrigation ditch to our right. We could use that. There are trees overhanging it, and it might offer better cover."

"Good spot to find an IED, too," Jacko pointed out.

Bluey pushed the talk button on his radio. "Trap Command, this is Bushranger One, over."

"Copy, Bushranger One."

"We're at Moonlight about to move to Ben Hall, over."

The team was using bushranger names for their waypoints as they moved on the target. Ben Hall was the compound and Jahan was Ned Kelly.

"Copy, Bushranger One."

"Is there any movement in the compound? Over."

"Negative."

"Roger that. Bushranger One, out."

Bluey looked at the vacant area before him and shook his head. Something was niggling at him deep down. "Bugger it. Jacko, take us into the ditch."

"Copy."

Jacko came to his feet and moved to his right, staying within the edge of the tree line. Bluey signaled to Lofty and said, "Set up here and cover us. Keep an eye on that compound. Once we reach the perimeter, I'll have you rejoin. But come along the ditch."

"Copy, boss."

Lofty found himself a reasonably flat position and laid down, using the scope on the 417 to watch the compound.

Bluey moved to the right following the rest of his team. To the north, the gunfire ebbed and flowed. The WHOP-WHOP-WHOP of a helicopter reached out through the clear blue sky. The Australian slipped into the cool water of the ditch, and it reached up to his thighs. Behind him came Red, the big, unassuming Victorian from outside of Bendigo.

"I hate walking through shit like this," he said in a low voice. "You never know if a fucking bunyip might bite your dick off."

Bluey smiled and shook his head. A bunyip was a mythical creature said to inhabit the waters of billabongs in inland Australia. "Poor thing would starve if he was looking for a feed of yours," Bluey said.

"That ain't what your missus said."

The team leader chuckled. This was how they dealt with high-stress situations; ribbing and humor.

"Bushranger, hold."

Lofty's voice was short, clipped.

"What is it, Lofty?"

"We have movement in the compound. I saw two fighting-aged males having a peek over the wall."

"Copy."

Bluey looked along the drain and saw Jacko low in the water. There was probably a further forty meters to reach the target. All four men waited with bated breath for the all clear.

"Bluey, one of these blokes has a sat phone."

"Shit. OK, keep an eye on him. Don't kill the bastard yet."

"Copy."

"Jacko, keep moving."

Suddenly, there was a sharp crack from a weapon then the snap as the round passed close overhead. "Shit!" Bluey exclaimed. "Jacko, go! Move forward."

Almost immediately, more gunshots started to pepper their position. Above them, bullets clipped branches and leaves from the trees. Others hammered into the banks of the ditch, kicking up dirt. "Lofty, find that fucking sniper. We'll take care of the others."

"Copy, Bluey."

"Red, lay down some fire on that wall."

The SAS man in front of Bluey stopped and raised his M4. He aimed at the mud-built wall and began laying down suppressing fire along it. The other three pressed forward. They reached the wall, and Bluey snapped more orders. "Red, come up. Ringa, put a frag over the wall."

The SAS man unhooked a fragmentation grenade, pulled the pin, and tossed it over the wall. "Frag out!"

With a loud crump, the grenade detonated and showered dirt and debris everywhere. "Ringa, wait for Red. Lofty, you found that bloody sniper yet?"

"Working on it."

"OK, Jacko, over you go," Bluey snapped. Then he said to Ringa, "When Red gets here, follow us."

"Roger that."

"Trap Command, we're at Ben Hall. Moving to Ned Kelly."

Both men climbed over the mud wall and dropped down on the other side. They remained in position for a moment while they scanned the interior of the compound. On the ground in front of Bluey was a fighting-aged male with an AK beside him. The grenade had done its job and shattered the man's frame, and his clothes were all bloodied.

Bluey took up the point position, and Jacko fell in behind him. From the recce photos, they knew that the main building was at the center of the compound, with smaller courtyards surrounded by other living quarters. Each of these was divided by narrow alleys, which could become a death trap if the team was caught in them.

In the first of the alleys, Bluey had made it halfway when an insurgent appeared. The man was surprised at the sight of the two Australians and froze. The M4 in Bluey's grasp spat a 5.56 slug which punched into the man's chest. To make sure, the Australian fired another hot on the heels of the first. He stepped over the fallen Taliban and peered around the corner of the building, to find a closed wooden gate blocking their path.

The pair could hear the rattle of gunfire emanating from the other side. Two, maybe three shooters. There was movement behind Jacko as Red and Ringa caught up with them. Bluey took one of his own grenades and pulled the pin. He tossed it over the wall and waited for the detonation.

As soon as it blew, he kicked the gate open and rushed through.

The courtyard was littered with human debris: buckets, household junk, old rags. Now joining the wreckage were two insurgents, one missing an arm and part of a leg. He'd obviously taken the brunt of the explosive force of the grenade. Beside him, another man squirmed from the pain of fragments lodged in his back.

The third shooter was still upright, and the AK in his hands fired a burst of 7.62 rounds in their direction. Bluey felt the heat of their passing but never flinched. He squeezed the trigger three times, and the Taliban jerked wildly under each impact.

Falling to the ground, the man didn't move. Using hand signals, Bluey directed Red and Ringa to clear the building on their left while he and Jacko did the same to the one on their right.

The one on the left was quickly cleared, and when they joined Bluey and Jacko, they found the pair looking over a virtual treasure trove of AK-47s, RPGs, unexploded shells, and countless boxes of ammunition. Obviously, it was Jahan's store.

Suddenly, Bluey's comms crackled to life. "Bushranger One, we've got a bolter out the back."

"Put him down, Lofty."

A moment of silence was replaced by, "Target down."

The team pushed on towards the compound's main building. They traversed a narrow alley and broke out into another courtyard. It was much the same as the previous one, littered with human debris.

It was then that Bluey realized that the firing had stopped and been replaced by the barking of a dog. The target building was larger than the others. He motioned Jacko forward, and the SAS man crossed to a solid looking wood door. He tried it and found it locked.

"Blow it," Bluey snapped.

Red moved forward and placed an EDX breaching charge on the door. Once he was done, he moved to one side and waited for Bluey. The team leader reached out and squeezed his shoulder.

Red triggered the explosion blowing the door in with a cloud of dust, wood splinters, and mortar. Ringa was the first man through into what looked to be a small anteroom. With that cleared, the team set about doing the same with the rest of the house. When they were finished, they looked at each other. Ringa asked, "Where the hell is he?"

Bluey pushed his talk button. "Lofty, copy?"

"Copy."

"How's it look out there?"

"All quiet, Boss."

"I want you to check that bolter and see if he's our HVT. Then come to us. Watch out for IEDs."

"Copy that."

The next call was to base. "Trap Command? Bushranger One, over."

"Copy, Bushranger One."

"Ned Kelly is not on site, I say again, Ned Kelly is not on site. Awaiting further orders."

"Copy, Bushranger One. Wait. Over."

A moment later, the voice came back. "Bushranger One,

do one more sweep of the compound, and then move to extract, over."

"Copy. Out."

Bluey turned to his men. "All right, let's do another sweep of the compound. Once we're done, we're to move to extract. Once we're outside, I'll call in a strike to blow the hell out of this place. Jacko, make a list of the shit we found in that building in the other courtyard."

The next twenty minutes were spent going through the compound room by room and hole by hole all for the result of a big fat zip. Or so Bluey thought.

He was just about to call them all together when Ringa called him. "Bluey, you have to come and see this. I'm behind the main house."

They all gathered there, Lofty included. His bolter had been another fighting-aged male but not their HVT. Ringa pointed at the ground. "We've got ourselves a tunnel."

The entrance was mostly covered, with only a slight sliver visible. "I take it that you haven't had a look yet?"

"Nope."

"Red, check it for wires," Bluey ordered and then started to strip his webbing off.

"You going down there, Bluey?" Jacko asked.

"That's the plan."

"That's just crazy, Boss."

"You aren't the one going."

Ringa stepped forward. "You need to give this some thought, Bluey. If the Taliban come back while you're down there, you've had the Richard."

His leader gave him a wry smile. "If the Taliban come back while I'm down there, I'll have had more than the dick. Just keep in contact with HQ, and they'll keep you up to date. Lofty, you and Red get up on a rooftop and pull security."

"OK, Boss."

Bluey took out his Glock 19 and checked there was round in the chamber. He then took out his small flashlight and said to Jacko, "Open her up."

With Ringa and Bluey covering the hole, Jacko pulled the cover back.

The opening had been gouged out through the tough crust just wide enough for a man to climb into the tunnel below. Bluey dropped to his knees and leaned down to make sure the entrance was clear. The smell of stale air wafted into his nostrils, but he ignored the stink and shone the flashlight beam around.

Below the surface, the tunnel was large enough for a man to traverse it, albeit in a crouched position. The SAS man came back up and looked at his men. "It's clear."

Bluey swung his legs over the hole and said, "See you blokes later."

"Watch your ass."

Once down in the tunnel, the smell grew almost over-powering due to lack of ventilation, and Bluey stopped to adjust before moving off. He ran a hand down one of the walls and nodded his appreciation at the time-consuming effort that had gone into excavating the passage through solid earth.

He started along the tunnel at a slow, deliberate pace. If he rushed, he could easily be killed, and who knew whether there was an IED in place.

Bluey edged forward until he came to a turn. He pointed the flashlight around first. Nothing like a bright light to blind a person. Then he took a deep breath and edged his head around to have a look.

"Ah fuck!" he cried out and lunged backward. The snarling bark of a savage dog echoed throughout the tunnel but was soon drowned out by the roar of an IED which the animal tripped.

Then everything went black.

——————

The ringing in his ears hurt like a bitch, but at least he was still alive. He had to be because surely you couldn't feel this much pain if you were dead. Bluey opened his eyes and saw Jacko leaning over him. Through the buzz in his ears, he heard a muffled, "You're a lucky bastard, Bluey. You know that?"

"What?"

Jacko said something to Ringa, and they helped him to his feet. Bluey's head swam, and he thought for a moment he might fall over. He looked down and saw his clothes covered in dust. Then he remembered the dog and the trip-wire in front of it.

"The dog?"

"Yeah, it's blown to shit, mate," Ringa said. "You were lucky you were around the corner, or you'd be strawberry jam too. As it was, the tunnel came down on you. Thanks to Jacko you're still alive. He dug you out."

Bluey was still stunned but was starting to come good. Even his hearing was returning slowly. "Let's get out of here. And thanks, Jacko."

Bluey got his kit back on, and they began their exfil. He wasn't happy about missing their target. But they were all still alive, so that was a bonus.

"Trap Command? Bushranger One, over."

"Copy, Bushranger One."

"We're headed for extract, expect to be on site in thirty mikes. No joy on Ned Kelly."

"Copy, Bushranger One. See you when you get back. Out."

That was it? See you when you get back? Shit.

"OK, Jacko, get us out of here."

"Copy that."

———

Tarin Kowt
Afghanistan

Bluey entered the comfort of the air-conditioned tent, looking for his commanding officer, Colonel Terry Power. When he found it empty, he turned around and was about to walk out when the colonel appeared at the doorway. "Clark, you're here. Good."

"Yes, sir."

"Bad luck about Jahan. Still, all your team came home."

"Yes, sir."

"I'm afraid you've got a new mission."

"So soon, sir?"

Power nodded. "You and your team have just enough time to get cleaned up, pack your kit, and catch the flight out of here."

"Where are we going, sir?"

"Italy."

CHAPTER 16

Piacevole Valley, Italy

"Bushranger One to Zero, over."

"Copy, Bushranger One."

"Zero, Bushranger Team is down and intact. We're just about to move towards the target."

"Roger that, Bushranger One. You have five hours to get into position. Be aware that the town is full of tangos."

"We've got this, sir. We'll be in position by the time your men arrive."

"Copy, Bushranger One. Zero out."

Bluey's team had dropped into the valley twenty minutes before. On the way down, he'd seen the high peaks of the surrounding mountains, standing sentinel over the landscape.

On touch down, they'd hidden their excess equipment and set up a perimeter while Bluey reported to Ferrero. The Australians had been surprised at the request for their help. Bluey thought that SEALs would have been more appropriate with it being an American op, instead of the SAS. But he'd been told that his team had been specifically asked for.

Every briefing had been via a computer screen whilst they'd been on the move, the final one in the air just before they'd jumped. Their mission was simple. Infiltrate the town and provide support to Kane, with one man tasked to eliminate Amando Bellandi.

"Jacko, time to move out. I want to be in that town an hour before daylight."

"Copy, boss."

Like wraiths, they moved silently through the night, Jacko guiding their way to the village. The valley was quiet, and the early morning hours were cold. Then appearing from the darkness on a hillside before them was a series of stone buildings. Bluey called a halt so they could rest before infiltrating the town.

"Right, you blokes, we do this quietly. We sneak in and leave no footprint. Once there, we lay low until it's time. Got it?"

They all nodded, and then Bluey took out a map of the village and a small light. He illuminated the drawing and pointed to a point on it. "This is where the bad guy lives. From what I can gather, this is where the exchange will take place."

He stabbed at more points on the sketch with his finger. "Lofty, you're here. You should get a clear field of fire from there. Red, Ringa, here and here. Once again, the coverage should be good. Jacko and I will work our way around the back of the building and infil when the time is right. Remember, we make their man the priority at all times. Whatever happens, he stays alive."

"Roger that."

———

On the Road

The SUV took the turn at a slower pace than the last. The bend switched back upon itself before straightening and then doing the same again in the opposite direction.

"Man, I hate roads like this in the dark," Axe said for the tenth time. "Especially when I ain't driving."

"You scared of the dark, Axe?" Kane asked.

"You know I ain't, Reaper. But shit, if we go off road here, it's about five hundred feet down the damned side of the mountain."

"Quick trip."

There was a moment's silence before Axe said, "You think these Aussies will come through for us?"

"If there's something I know about these Aussies, they'll do what they say they will. Just like in Somalia."

Axe said, "I hope the plan works out for them."

It wasn't much of a plan, other than infiltrating the village and take up covering positions. Although Kane did tell Bluey to get into the house and have a look around if he could. "They'll be fine."

———

Piacevole Valley
Italy

"That's it there, boss, on the side of that hill," Jacko told Bluey.

They hunkered down while Bluey studied their target through night vision optics. The glasses showed some well-maintained homes as well as shacks that were lucky to be still standing, and a number of washing lines with loose strands of wire hanging from them. After several minutes of taking everything in, he said, "All right. This is it. Remember, no footprint. Lofty, once you're in that bell tower, radio in. The same goes for the rest of you. Any questions?"

No one said a word.

"OK then ..."

"What if we have to kill someone?" Red asked.

"Hide the body somewhere safe and pray that it isn't noticed."

"OK."

"Anything else?"

Nothing.

"Let's go."

What they did next wasn't really to a team's strength. They were used to working together as a unit, not individual units. But they'd been trained to adapt when the situation called for it, which was what they were doing now.

At the edge of the village, Bluey and Jacko came across the first stone-built building constructed in medieval times. It was dark and cold against the moonlit sky; the holes that had once held windows stood out like dark eyes.

The cobbled street before them sloped upward and curved around the hill perhaps fifty meters further on. They walked up the sidewalk, making sure that every step was taken with care.

"Hold up," Bluey said to Jacko.

The SAS man stopped and took a knee, his M4 up at his shoulder. "What's up?"

"I have movement at our twelve."

They waited and watched. And then a guard moved from behind a protruding bush. Through their NVGs, they could see he was armed with some form of an automatic weapon. "What do you want to do?" Jacko asked.

"We go around."

They waited for the man to return to his position behind the bush before Bluey ran across the street then took up a firing position while Jacko followed. After checking for further movement, they worked their way through an overgrown yard then on to the next street farther up the slope.

Bluey's comms crackled to life. "Bushranger Two in position."

Through the darkened shadows of the eerily quiet street, Bluey and Jacko moved like wraiths. Again, the SAS team leader's comms crackled to life. "Bushranger Four in position."

Which left Lofty, who shouldn't be far away.

Shouldn't, but things have a way of biting you on the ass at the least opportune moment.

————

"Non muoverti cazzo," a harsh voice snarled, and Lofty felt the hard barrel of a gun press against the back of his neck.

"You've got to be kidding me," the Australian growled in a low voice.

"English? Turn around."

Lofty did as he was told and said, "Na, mate. I'm bloody Australian."

"Australian?"

"Yeah, cobber."

"Drop your gun," the man snapped.

Lofty lay the 417 gently on the ground. He straightened and said, "What now?"

"We go and see Mister Bellandi."

Lofty shook his head. "Afraid I can't do that, Cobber. It would ruin everything."

"What?"

The SAS man just smiled at him, which seemed to piss him off. "Turn around."

Lofty did as he was asked.

"Now, move."

He didn't.

The guard leaned in to give Lofty a shove. Mistake.

The SAS man whirled about as the hand touched him. His left hand knocked the gun from the Italian's hand while his right hand drove into the man's throat, cutting off all possible noise such as a sudden shout of surprise.

A direct blow from Lofty's left fist caught the man on the bridge of the nose causing him to stagger back. Not giving the man time to recover his senses, the SAS warrior drew his knife and drove it up under the Italian's chin. As it pierced the palette and into the man's brain, Lofty felt the rush of hot blood and cerebrospinal fluid flow over his knife hand. He quickly hefted the dead man's weight before it fell to the ground, dragging him back into the bushes to conceal him. Retrieving the gun, he disabled it, laying it beside the dead man. Then Lofty bent down and collected his own 417.

Cursing under his breath, he pressed his transmit button. "Bushranger One? Bushranger Five. We have a small problem. Over."

There was a long pause, and Bluey's voice filled his ear. "Go ahead, Lofty."

"I got rumbled by a guard. He's out of action now, but I'm just letting you know."

"Roger that. Proceed with your mission."

"Copy. Five out."

Although the words were not spoken, the SAS man knew that his team leader was far from happy. And after the mission was complete, he was betting that he'd hear all about it.

After finally reaching his destination, Lofty found the door to the old church open. Easing himself through the opening, he then moved into the void beyond. Through the green haze of his NVGs, the SAS man could see the rows of disused pews laid out before him. He walked along the main aisle, scraps of paper and grass littered along its length until he reached the altar. From there, he walked through a doorway and found the stairs, which led up into the bell tower.

Every step was slow and tedious as Lofty tested each tread before putting his full weight upon it. When he reached the summit, he set up his hide and radioed Bluey to let him know that he was in position.

———

"Bushranger Five in position."

"Copy that."

Bluey was dark that his man had been discovered, but he needed to push that aside and hope that no one noticed the missing man. He adjusted his position and then said into his mic, "Zero? Bushranger One, copy?"

"Copy, Bushranger One."

"All call signs in position. Just waiting for dawn's early light to execute the last part."

"Roger that. Any problems?"

"Nothing we couldn't handle. Bushranger One, out."

Bluey looked down at his watch. "We'll give it another hour, and we'll breach. Reaper should be arriving about then, and they'll be looking the other way. I'll take first watch. Get some kip."

"You don't have to tell me twice," Jacko said and hunkered down to make himself comfortable.

While Jacko slept, Bluey sat almost motionless, watching, waiting.

––––––––

Beneath Museo Gregoriano Egiziano
Vatican City

The screams that had echoed throughout the crypt for most of the night finally died away, and Cara's frayed nerves were thankful for the respite, a small mercy. The sudden silence did her no favors as it was then that doubts began to snake their tendrils in to plague her mind. The new surroundings were cold and damp, which made her previous accommodation seem luxurious. Her captivity had been going on for so long that she wondered whether her team would ever come and secure her release.

No, don't think like that.

Another scream. This time it was different. Who would have thought that a place held in such high religious esteem could hide a place so dark and sinister? The people who haunted the dark, dimly-lit catacombs beneath the city posed as priests by day but were in fact far from it. They were Druids, the personification of evil, practicing human sacrifice, and interpreting omens.

It was a ghastly place, and although Cara had only been there for a couple of days, with her hands chained above her head by rusted manacles, it was already affecting her.

A shadow flitted across the wall, and a man appeared wearing a hooded cloak. The garment was white but stained with large splotches of blood. He stopped in front of Cara and said, "It will be your turn soon. When the moon is full, you will be sacrificed to the Gods. They are crying out for a strong gift like yourself."

The self-proclaimed druid reached out and traced a finger across Cara's stomach, feeling the taut muscles beneath the thin fabric of her dress as she flinched. A cold smile touched his lips, and his finger moved upwards, found a breast, and traced around her nipple, which responded to the touch. Then he took it between his thumb and forefinger and squeezed it gently. "It is a shame that such a fine specimen of womanhood should have to die, but the Gods' will must be done."

Cara's eyes narrowed. "I'm going to cut your heart out, asshole."

The man chuckled, let go of her nipple and then squeezed her breast. "Yes, a pity."

Cara strained against her bonds her jaw clenched. She lifted her right leg to kick him in the balls, but the chains around her legs snapped tight with a loud jingle. The man sneered at her and dropped his hand to his side.

"I see you can't sleep either tonight, Brother White," came a voice from behind the druid. The man turned to stare at another man dressed in an identical hooded cloak, minus the blood.

Cara stared at the man through the dim light. He was a

craggy-faced man, the lines on which appeared to be burn scars from the distant past. The man he referred to as Brother White said, "It must be one of those nights, Brother Red."

"It must be. I see that you've been busy."

White looked down at his blood-stained robe and said, "I had a dream. I wanted to see what the Gods had to say about it."

"Really? What was their message?"

"Nothing clear."

"Maybe you need to talk to them again? Maybe a second time will provide some clarity for you?"

White nodded. "Maybe, Brother."

"Which one of the poor wretches did you use in hope of getting answers?"

"The German one."

"And did you satisfy your need before you cut the poor bitch's throat?"

White smiled once more. "But of course."

"Asshole," Cara hissed.

White's face screwed up with anger, and his right hand shot out, grabbing Cara's breast once more. This time, however, instead of a gentle caress, he squeezed it cruelly, causing her to wince. Flecks of spittle flew from his lips as he said vehemently, "Your turn is coming, you bitch. I'll rip that dress from your body and make you scream for mercy as I pound you into oblivion."

"Remember yourself, Brother White!" Red snapped. "She is for the Gods, this one. There is a full moon in two more nights, and she shall be sacrificed on the altar from which they shall receive her spirit."

White composed himself and stepped back from Cara.

He bowed his head in remorse and said, "Forgive me, Brother. I forgot myself for a moment."

"Yes, you did," Red agreed. Then he reached into his cloak pocket and took out a small plastic bag with a fine white powder in it. "Maybe you need some of your medicine, Brother White. Maybe the answers you seek can be found within the dreams it induces."

Cara snorted when she realized what it was. "You're nothing but a fucking junkie. Hooked on what? Cocaine? Heroine? Your Gods must be so proud of you."

"You know nothing!" White screeched, a vein popping out on his forehead. As though to reinforce his message, he closed in on Cara, his face only inches from hers. Seizing the presented opportunity, she snapped her head forward, her brow smashing into the bridge of White's nose. Lights flashed in her head with the ferocity of the impact, and the druid reeled away with a howl of pain. Blood spurted then flowed freely, joining the blood already on his robe and, despite her own pain, Cara smiled when she caught sight of the damage she had wreaked.

"How'd you like that, you son of a bitch?" she asked, a smirk on her face.

"I'll fucking kill you!" White screamed, his voice echoing from the damp walls.

"Enough!" Red roared. "Get out of here, Brother, before I lose all patience with you."

Grumbling and wiping at the blood on his face, careful to avoid his ruined nose, White stalked off into the depths of the crypt. Red stared at Cara and said, "He will not be a forgiving man, I'm afraid."

"I don't care."

He studied her for a moment and then chuckled. "I see through your façade, my dear. You are scared, and you conceal it behind bravado. But don't worry, it will be over soon. Make your peace with God. I'm sure he will accept you with open arms."

With that, Brother Red disappeared into the gloom, leaving Cara shedding silent tears as her tough exterior crumbled.

CHAPTER 17

Bucolic, Piacevole Valley
Italy

"Bluey, wake up," Jacko said, shaking his team leader awake.

"What is it?"

"Time to go. Reaper One is due in soon."

Bluey looked at his watch and then at the lightening tinge in the eastern sky. He touched his talk button and said, "Bushranger Team, check in."

Each man responded in turn, indicating that everything was clear, then Bluey called Bravo.

"Copy, Bushranger One, this is Zero."

"Sitrep, please, Zero."

"At this point, all seems OK."

"Copy. We're about to move into position."

"Roger that. Good luck. ETA on Reaper One is ten minutes. Out."

"OK, Jacko, let's move."

The two men came out of their hide, and stealthily

approached the house. They climbed over an old stone wall and into the rear yard. Bluey took a knee and swept the area while Jacko moved up to the back door. A moment later, Bluey joined him and then said into his mic, "Bravo Three, copy?"

Teller's voice came over the net, "Copy, Bushranger One."

"What have we got with the house? Over."

"Our eye in the sky tells me that there are six people inside the house. At this point, you have four on the ground floor and two on the second. I suspect that one of them could be the package."

Bluey thought for a moment. "Zero, request permission to try for the package."

"Wait one, Bushranger."

"Waiting, out."

———

Just Outside Bucolic

"Reaper One, Copy?"

The SUV bumped over the unmaintained road, forcing Kane to slow. "Copy, Zero."

"Reaper, Bushranger One is requesting permission to go in after the package."

Kane glanced at Axe. The big man shrugged. "It may work," he told his team leader.

Kane nodded. Then he said, "Bushranger One, copy?"

"Copy."

"Sitrep?"

"I believe your friend is being held on the second floor

of the house with one guard watching over her. I say we can get her out without upsetting the apple cart."

"How certain are you?"

"You know about our game and certainty, Reaper. You could show up on their doorstep, and they could shoot her with you looking on. But I say our way is sound."

Kane still wasn't sure, but what he said next made sense to him. "Do it. We'll be onsite in five mikes."

"Copy. Bushranger One going hot."

"Good luck."

———

Bucolic, Piacevole Valley
Italy

"Bushranger One to all callsigns. Plan Beta, I say again, Plan Beta. Acknowledge."

"Copy that. Plan Beta," came the reply from every team member.

Each SAS man, except for Lofty, broke cover. He would stay in the old bell tower and watch over the rest like a clucky mother hen. The others would now perform the job with the military precision they'd been instilled with. "Bravo Three, I need you to call all targets to my men as you see them. You're about to become a busy man."

"Copy, Bushranger One. Calling targets."

In the background noise of his comms, Bluey heard Teller start to do just that for individual operators. Each one was answered with a tango down call. "Come on, Jacko; let's get in there."

The two men climbed onto the lower level roof and

then up to the second-floor window. Bluey took out his suppressed sidearm and tried the window. It was open. "Bushranger One is breaching."

"Copy, One, the room is clear," Teller responded.

The SAS team leader raised his right leg and slid it over the window ledge. Then he followed it with the other. Once inside, he quickly swept the small, sparsely-furnished bedroom. With no visible threats, he moved across to the door, his heavy boots silent on the floor. Bluey tried the doorknob. It turned freely, and he cracked the door to look out. The hallway on the other side was clear.

"Bushranger One, you have a mobile target approaching your position along the hallway."

Bluey froze. The fact that he couldn't see the tango meant that they were coming from the other direction. The SAS man stepped back from the door, leaving it ajar. He lifted the Glock 19 and waited. Behind him, Jacko had his M4 raised and ready.

"In Bluey's ear, Teller was whispering, "Hold. Hold. Hold. Now."

Just before that final word, Bluey heard the soft footfall just outside the door. The Glock fired twice, and the rounds punched through the wood. A grunt emanated from the other side of the door as the bullets buried deep into the man beyond. As he slumped to the floor, Bluey pulled the door open and swung it wide, stepping through the opening and bending to check the fallen man. There was no doubt; the man was dead.

"Tango down in the hall."

"Roger, One," Teller said. "If you go along the hall to your right, you'll find your next target in the room there."

With more than a modicum of stealth, the two men made their way along to the indicated door, and once again,

Bluey tried it while Jacko covered his back. This time, the door was locked, so the SAS man reached into his pocket and retrieved his lockpick.

Bluey placed the Glock beside his knee while he worked on the lock. A few moments later, it clicked open.

Bluey put the picks in his pocket and came to his feet. He opened the door and slipped inside with his gun up, ready to fire.

The room was dim, the early morning light beginning to filter through the thin curtains. In the center of the floor was a chair. On the chair sat a figure, with its back to them, a hood placed over its head.

Bluey said softly into his mic, "Zero, we've found the package. Just confirming that it is who we are after."

At the sound of their voices, the hooded head snapped around from side to side, a muffled noise coming through the material. Bluey crossed quickly to the figure, walked around in front, and reefed off the hood. It was definitely a woman, but not the one they wanted. It wasn't Cara.

"Zero, this is Bushranger One, copy?"

"Copy."

"The prisoner is not the package, I say again, not the package. Wait, out."

"Copy."

Bluey took the gag away from her mouth. "Who are you, Miss?"

"Tiffy. Are you here to rescue me?" she asked with an English accent.

"We're here for Cara. Do you know where she is?"

"Who?"

The SAS man shook his head. "Zero. This is a bust. We're going to secure the house and see if we can find someone who knows what the hell is going on."

"Roger that," Ferrero acknowledged.

"Come on, Jacko. Let's go and clear the rest of the house."

"Wait, you can't leave me here," Tiffy pleaded.

"We'll be back. I promise."

"At least untie me."

Bluey raised the gag back into place. "Safer for you if we don't."

The pair left the room, closing the door behind them and worked their way along the hall to the top of the stairs. When they found them to be clear, the team leader placed a heavy boot on the first step to test it. The wood appeared to be solid and made no sound.

On the ground floor, both men proceeded to clear each room on that level. When they reached the kitchen, one man was there brewing coffee, and they took him out quickly with two shots to the chest. Which left three tangos in the house.

Bluey followed Jacko through the door into the living room and found the three remaining people that had been unaccounted for. Two men and a woman. The largest man's reaction was a fraction too slow in bringing up the Steyr he was holding. Two bullets from Jacko's M4 punched into his chest, and he dropped to the slate floor in an untidy heap. The guard died choking on his own blood.

Bluey centered his sights on the chest of the other man who seemed to be frozen to the spot. Beside him, the woman began screaming and didn't stop until the man snapped something in Italian. Bluey said into his mic, "Zero, house is secure."

"Fucking Americans," the man hissed.

Jacko smiled at him. "No, mate, we're Australian."

"All callsigns, sitrep?" said Bluey.

The rest of the team called in one by one, informing their leader that everything was fine and all threats had been eliminated. Nodding, the team leader pressed his talk button once more. "Zero, village secure."

"Copy, Bushranger One. Good job."

Bluey passed his M4 over to Jacko and turned on Amando Bellandi. "Right, asshole, where's the woman?"

"Screw you."

"Wrong answer," Bluey said and slapped him across the face. "I ain't got time for your shit. Pretty soon Italian intelligence will be coming in here, and I'm almost certain they're going to put a bullet in your head. But before that, we're going to need answers."

Bellandi snorted. "Do you know who I am?"

"Mate, I don't give two shits who you are. All I want from you is the answer to my question."

Bellandi spit on Bluey's boot.

"OK, fine. Jacko, get the woman out of here."

"What do you want me to do with her, Boss?"

"Show her how much of a gentleman you can be."

"What are you going to do to me?" Elettra blurted out.

Jacko took her by the arm. "Get up."

"No."

He squeezed harder. "Get up."

The front door snapped open, and the void was filled by a solid figure, the face a mask of frustrated rage. Crossing the room to where Bellandi sat, an M17 came into his hand, and he placed the barrel against the killer's right knee. Without compunction, he squeezed the trigger blowing a bullet through the Italian's leg.

The Reaper had arrived.

———

Milan, Italy

Three CIA agents burst into the large room, looking around with troubled expressions on their faces. They found Thurston and snapped a few words in Italian. Immediately, she went into action. "Traynor, Arenas, on me. We've got tangos inbound. It looks like the prophecy has come true. The rest of you keep an eye on things."

The three of them left the room, followed by one agent, and out into the warehouse proper. They hurried across to the cage that served as their armory and immediately kitted up with vests and ammunition. "Do we know how far out they are?" she asked Crowe, the agent in charge.

"About a minute, Ma'am. They're in three SUVs."

"How did they find us?"

"They have eyes everywhere according to Efisio Capello. I guess what he actually means is they have someone on the inside."

Thurston nodded. "I'd like to find out who."

Joined by the other two CIA agents and Bravo elements, the Reaper team members jogged towards the main doors of the warehouse. Thurston was thankful that they were there, especially after past events.

They exited the building, and the general noticed that Arenas had scooped up a 110A1. He raced across to one of the SUVs and set up. Then he waited the thirty seconds that it took for the first vehicle to appear. A BMW X5 followed by two more. Arenas squeezed the trigger, and the 110 slammed back into his shoulder. The 7.62mm slug punched through the front screen and smashed into the driver's face, killing him instantly. The vehicle pulled left at speed and slammed into a concrete wall.

Arenas shifted his aim to the second SUV and fired again. It left the road and hit a dirt embankment, rolling onto its side, its rear end kicking around, blocking the path of the one behind it.

"That stopped the bastards," Traynor snapped and opened fire at the shooters starting to scramble from the vehicles, with the 416 he was holding.

"I can't stand *gilipollas*," Arenas cursed, picking off a Steyr-wielding Italian.

The intruders began to return fire from behind the upturned vehicles, and the SUV where Arenas was leaning, tapped out a staccato beat as bullets punched through its panels and doors, creating a Swiss cheese effect. He slipped back down behind the engine block, using its solidity as cover. "Mama ain't going to be happy about this," he said out loud.

"What was that?" Thurston asked from beside him.

"Nice day, Ma'am."

"I bet," she growled as she rose, letting loose a long burst of gunfire.

Another fusillade of shots brought a shooter to his knees with holes stitched across his chest. Then it all stopped. The remaining men threw down their weapons and raised their hands in surrender.

The team moved quickly but cautiously, securing the prisoners with cable ties to be held for Italian intelligence to pick up. Arenas checked over each of the vehicles to make sure everything was secure. As he came to the dead driver of the first vehicle to arrive, he recognized Carlo Laurito. His first bullet had punched the man's ticket well and truly.

"How are we looking?" Thurston asked.

"All clear in here, Ma'am," he said.

"Good. It was lucky we had sufficient warning to respond."

Thurston went back inside still carrying her 416 and wearing her vest. Ferrero stared at her and asked, "How was it?"

"Just like old times. How's everything going with Reaper?"

"I think we may be getting somewhere. I'm just waiting for him to check in."

Piacevole Valley
Italy

"What is he doing still alive?" Capello snapped upon seeing Bellandi sitting in the chair, holding his bloody leg.

"Because we had to question him, that's why," Kane said.

"Well, kill him now," the Italian ordered.

"We aren't finished with him yet."

"Are you afraid that I might tell them something, Efisio?" Bellandi sneered.

"Shut up," Capello snapped.

Kane glanced at Bluey questioningly.

"Come on, Efisio, you know I won't stay in jail, and when I get out, I'll pay my old friend a visit."

Suddenly a weapon appeared in Capello's hand.

"No!" Kane shouted, but it was too late. The sidearm crashed, and the bullet it expelled punched into the killer's head.

Kane whirled on the Italian. "What the fuck did you do that for? I needed him to answer some more questions."

"He would not answer them," answered the man, matter-of-factly.

"I'll never find out now, will I?"

Capello remained mute, so Kane glanced at Bluey and nodded. The SAS man left the room and returned a few moments later with a struggling Elettra Bellandi. At the sight of her husband, she reefed herself from her captor's hands, screeched and threw herself at the dead man, burying her face into his chest. Kane grabbed her by the arm and pulled her away from her husband. "I need to ask you some questions."

She turned to look at Kane and caught sight of Capello. Her face twisted in rage. "You did this. You did this because he would have exposed your dirty little secret."

"What are you talking about?" Capello hissed. "Shut up."

But the woman wouldn't be silenced. "Maybe I will tell it instead now that you have killed him."

With a snarl, Capello drew his gun again and raised it to fire. Once more, the sound of a gunshot filled the room.

Capello stiffened and turned to stare at Bluey. His eyes were asking the question his mouth could not. The SAS man lowered the weapon, and he said, "I figure you shooting one person cold is enough, Enzo. You don't get to do it again."

The Italian fell to the floor, dead.

Kane asked Elettra, "Why did he want to kill you?"

"Because he worked for my husband."

"He was a mole?"

"Yes."

"I'm still looking for my friend. Your husband said she was sent away. Where?"

"What is in it for me?"

Kane stared at her. "I will let you go."

She snorted with laughter. "I do not believe you."

"I guess it's all you have. If you don't tell me, I'll turn you over to Italian intelligence."

Fear flared in her eyes. "At least my way," Kane said, "there's a possibility of you getting out of Italy before the Mafia gets you."

"OK," she said, "I will tell you."

"Good. Spill it. And don't leave anything out."

"She is in Vatican City."

"Oh shit," Bluey said. "That's a whole different world."

"You've been there before?" Kane asked.

The SAS man nodded. "Yeah, me and some of the guys worked with the Special Swiss Guard, training them in special tactics, counter-terrorism, and other shit like that."

Kane frowned. "I never knew they had something like that."

"They don't. Not officially anyway. But with this whole ISIS bullshit that was going on in Europe, they wanted a force specially to guard the Pope. They originally wanted British SAS counter-terror to do it, but they had something on at the time and passed it off to us."

"What's she doing in Vatican City?" Kane asked.

"She was taken to the Brotherhood."

"What brotherhood?"

"The Brotherhood of Druids."

Bluey shook his head in disbelief. "You're having a fucking lark, love."

"A what?"

"A joke. You're joking. They're not real, just a myth."

"They are real," Elettra snapped.

"You've heard of these guys, Bluey?" Kane asked.

"When we were there training the Swiss Guard. I always thought it was just some bullshit story. You know, a suburban legend. Especially the bit about them practicing human sacrifice."

"Shit, what?"

"It's true," Elettra said. "They take the girls that are of no use anymore. The Druids are seriously fucked up."

"What does that say about you?" Kane asked. "You delivered the girls to them."

"Not me, Amando."

"No difference."

Elettra remained silent.

"How do we find them?"

"I don't know."

"How, damn it?"

"*I don't know!*"

"I might know of a way," mused Bluey.

Kane glanced at him. "Feel like taking a trip?"

"Sure, why not?"

———

Milan, Italy

"If you think I'm going to let the team loose in Vatican City, then think again," Thurston growled.

"It's the only way we'll damned well find Cara, General," Kane pointed out more than a little forcefully.

"Turn it down a notch, Gunny," she cautioned him. "I'm on your side, remember?"

"I agree, Ma'am," Bluey said.

"Excuse me?"

Kane shot a scorching glare at the Australian who ignored him. "I was saying, Ma'am, that it would be a bad idea having your whole team inside Vatican City. But maybe two people might be better off."

"Are you willing to go in there unarmed?"

"Like –"

"Yes, Ma'am," Bluey cut him off.

"Fine. But on the surface, this must have zero footprint."

"What about below the surface?"

"Waste the bastards."

"I can deal with that."

"So, just to clarify things, you're green-lighting the op, Ma'am?" Kane asked.

"Yes."

"That's a relief," Bluey said. "Because I have already set up a meeting for tomorrow with a contact who can fill us in on the blokes we're after."

"I guess we'd better get packed up, then if you want to make that meeting tomorrow."

"Yes, Ma'am."

Once out of earshot, Kane said to Bluey, "Who's your contact?"

"He's one of the men I helped train with the Swiss Guard. Funny thing is, he's a Brit. Don't ask me how he ended up there. I've no idea. He's good people, though."

"Do you think he will be able to help?"

"I sure hope so."

CHAPTER 18

Beneath Museo Gregoriano Egiziano
Vatican City

The following day dawned bright and fresh. The sky was clear, and the breeze was cool. By eight, Rome was buzzing with vehicles and tourists, the latter having made the pilgrimage to the ancient city to hear and see Pope Michael – if only from a distance - who was to make a speech in Vatican City the following morning. People had traveled from every corner of the globe to be part of the congregation, which the Brotherhood of Druids intended to make use of. They planned to make a statement.

The sacrifices over the past few days had been leading up to that point which, with precise timing, would culminate with the final sacrifice and The Event. The Event was what it was all about. The sacrifice of the strong one, the Oracle had said, would drain the strength from her body and transfer it to the Chosen One, helping him to succeed in his mission.

Cara had heard whispers about the ones the brothers called the Oracle and the Chosen One.

"Is this her?" a voice said, echoing from the stone walls of the catacombs.

Cara opened her eyes and saw Brother Red standing there beside another man she'd not seen before. He looked nothing like the druids that she'd already seen. This man was younger and fitter than the others and was dressed in white braided with gold.

Brother Red nodded. "Yes, your grace. This is her. She is strong; the gods will be pleased."

The man nodded. "But I see you are troubled. What is the problem?"

"She has friends who are looking for her, and they are coming to the city."

Cara's eyes flickered at the mention of her friends, but she said nothing. Instead, it was the new man who spoke. "What is being done to take care of them?"

"It is under control."

"I hope so. Nothing is to stop us from our course."

Cara chuckled.

"What is so funny?" the newcomer asked.

"If my friends are coming, asshole, they'll kill you."

"Show the bishop some respect," Brother Red hissed.

"Screw you."

"Easy, Brother Red. She is scared. It is fine."

Cara shook her head and let her pent-up fear turn to anger. "I ain't scared, you prick. I'm excited. Because my friends are going to cut your fucking heart out."

Red stepped forward, and Cara cringed. However, the bishop stopped him. "Leave it. We shall go."

As both men walked off into the shadows and their footsteps faded, Cara was left on her own with only her chains for company.

———

Rome, Italy

They planned to meet at a small, out of the way café with a stone façade. Bluey and Kane had arrived early and were now drinking strong coffee, waiting patiently for the Australian's contact to reach out. "He shouldn't be far away," Bluey said, looking at his watch.

Both men were unarmed and dressed casually in jeans and collared shirts. Kane watched a young couple walk by holding hands, smiling, oblivious to the troubles of the world.

"Do you think they know?" Kane asked.

"Know what?"

"That life isn't all beer and skittles."

"They'll find out one day."

The waiter approached their table once more and asked whether they would like a refill, to which both men agreed. "Are you sure your guy is coming?" Kane asked impatiently.

"He said he was."

Another ten minutes passed before a tall, broad-shouldered man appeared, dressed in cargo pants and a blue shirt. He flashed them a smile and said in a heavy accent said, "Sorry I'm late; I had some things to take care of."

Bluey introduced him to Reaper, and the men shook hands. Craig Fletcher, late of the "Regiment", now headed up the Swiss Guards Special Team.

"What can I do for you, chaps?" he asked, pulling out a chair and sitting down.

"We need your help, Fletch," Bluey explained. "We're trying to locate a missing woman somewhere in Vatican City."

Fletcher nodded. "I'll help where I can. What's her name?"

"Cara Billings."

The man nodded. "You got more, Bluey?"

They gave him a basic rundown of events and then dropped the bombshell about the druids. "Word is the druids have her."

Fletcher stared at them both in bewilderment. "You two are having a laugh, right?"

When they said nothing, he shook his head. "You're not."

"We got the information straight from the source," Bluey told him.

"Whoever that was lied to you."

"I don't think so," Kane said.

"Come on, Fletch. You were the one who told me about all this bullshit in the first place," the Australian reminded him.

"Only as a laugh. This shit isn't real."

"Can you help us or not?" Kane asked, starting to get annoyed. "She's here, and we'll go at it whether you do or not."

Fletcher's gaze chilled. "That's not a good idea, friend."

"I don't much care whether it is or not. She's one of mine, and she's not being left behind."

The Brit studied him for a moment and then sighed. "I'll see what I can come up with. Give me until tomorrow afternoon."

Kane didn't like it but nodded anyway. "All right then. We'll wait."

"I'll give you a call."

The man rose from his seat and walked off. Kane looked across the table at Bluey and saw the troubled expression on his face. "What's wrong?"

"I'm not sure. The Fletch I knew once would have jumped over the table to help out. But somehow, he's different now."

"The responsibility of command will do that."

The Australian smiled and shrugged. "Isn't that the truth?"

"Come on, we'll head back to the safehouse."

———

Safehouse, Rome

"How did it go?" Ferrero asked upon their return.

Kane shrugged. "I'm not sure. Bluey reckons that there was something off about his friend."

Ferrero looked in the Australian's direction. "How off?"

"I'm not sure. He hasn't seen him for some years, but still, something wasn't right."

"So, what did he say?"

"That he'd ask around and get back to us tomorrow afternoon," Bluey said. "That was after he tried to brush us off."

"So now we wait?" Ferrero asked.

"No, we can't," Swift said, appearing from another room. "I think I might have something else. Something more troubling."

"What do you mean?" Kane asked.

"Gwynn ap Nudd," Swift said.

"Who's he?"

"The Druid's God of war, death, fallen warriors, the hunt. King of the Sidhe and the Otherworld. Nasty piece of work by all belief. The Celts used to sacrifice to him before they went into battle or something big was to happen. They would conduct the sacrifices over a few days and then leave the strongest one for last."

"Is there a point to this?" Ferrero asked.

"Over the past four days, the local police have found the bodies of four young ladies scattered around Rome. Each one had had their throat slashed."

"You think they're connected?" Kane asked.

"I did a little digging and found that two years ago the same thing happened and then an attempt was made on the Pope's life. It failed, but only by dumb luck. There were five bodies found around the time of the attempt. Back in eighty-two when Pope Francis the Fourth was assassinated, five girls were found. If you go back even further to the mid-fifties, another five women were found with their throats slashed. At that time, another attempt was made on a sitting pope. It failed because the gun did not discharge. You see the pattern?"

"You're telling us that something is about to happen?" Kane asked. "That Cara could be the fifth one?"

Swift nodded. "Each time the Fifth woman was found, it was after the event, which makes me believe that they are killed around the time it is supposed to happen."

"Why would they do that?" Ferrero asked.

"Because they believe that the strength of the strongest one is passed on."

"They're going after the Pope?" Bluey theorized.

"That would be my guess," Swift said with a nod.

"If that's the case, where?"

"He has an open-air mass tomorrow at eleven," Swift told them.

"Which means we have got until then to find Cara," Kane said.

"Sorry, Reaper," the computer tech apologized.

"Not your fault. We need a place to start looking."

"But where?" Bluey said. "Rome is a big city."

"No, not Rome," Swift said hurriedly. "I'd say they want to be close. Maybe Vatican City itself."

"Still going to be like looking for a needle in a haystack," Bluey observed.

"There might be a way. There is a curator at one of the museums who's been around for a while. He's apparently into all kinds of alternative religious stuff."

"What is his name?" Ferrero asked.

"Professor Callisto Bianchi."

"Where's he at?"

"A place called *Museo Gregoriano Egiziano*," Swift rattled off, looking proud of his pronunciation.

Bluey snorted. "That's a frigging mouthful."

"It's a place to start," Kane said. "If we wait for your mate, I think we'll be too late."

"You'll have to go back in unarmed," Ferrero said.

"We still need to warn someone about what we think is going to happen," Kane told Ferrero.

"But what will happen? We have nothing except theories. The best we can do is put some people in the crowd and hope it turns out OK."

———

Museo Gregoriano Egiziano
Vatican City, Italy

Professor Callisto Bianchi was seated behind his desk when the knock came on his door. He put down the pen he was making notes with and looked up. "*Entra.*"

Kane and Bluey entered the through the light wood door and found a thin-faced man, with gray hair and brown eyes behind wire-framed spectacles. "*Posso aiutarti in qualche modo?*"

"Sorry, what?" Kane asked.

The professor smiled apologetically. "I'm sorry. Let me start again. How can I help you?"

"My name is John Kane. My friend is Bluey Clarke. We'd like to ask you a few questions if we may?"

"Certainly. Come in and close the door." The man gestured with his hands.

After Bluey had closed the door, both men crossed to a couple of chairs on the opposite side off the desk. Once seated, Kane said, "Professor, we were told that you are the man to come to about alternative religious beliefs. Is that true?"

Bianchi nodded tentatively. "I study the alternatives, amongst other things. Which one are you interested in?"

"Druids," Bluey told him.

He stared at them for a moment before asking, "What would you like to know?"

"Where we could find them in Vatican City?" Kane asked.

"Druids?"

"Yes."

"In Vatican City?"

"Yes."

"What makes you think that they are here?"

Bluey was growing impatient. "Are they here or not? You're the joker who studies this shit."

The indignant professor rose from his seat. "Gentlemen —"

"Ease up, Professor," Kane said before he could ask them to leave. "Just hear us out and then make up your mind."

Bianchi nodded hesitantly, then retook his seat. "All right. Speak your piece."

For the next few minutes, the professor listened intently to what they had to say. When the two men were finished, he shook his head in disbelief. "You say that all of these incidents coincide with the deaths of these women?"

Kane nodded. "Every one of them."

"And you think that your friend will be a sacrifice and that an attempt will be made on the pope's life tomorrow?"

"Pretty much, yes."

Bianchi chuckled. "That is a fantastic story, gentlemen. Fantastic indeed. Maybe a mere coincidence."

"Too much of a coincidence, if you ask me," Bluey said.

"Have you told anyone about this?"

They shook their heads. "What would we say?"

The professor looked thoughtful for a moment, and Kane noticed the change. "What is it?"

"I want to show you something."

"Like what?"

"Well, at first, I thought you might be here to make fun of my research. After all, you wouldn't be the first, but after what you've just told me, I think you are maybe here for legitimate reasons."

"Damn right, we are," Bluey said.

"There is a place," Bianchi said. "It is under the museum. Not many people know about it. There is an altar."

"How is it meant to help us?"

"It might give you an idea or clue where to look next."

The two men shrugged. At that point in time, they were willing to try anything. The three men walked out into the hallway. Bianchi stopped suddenly. "I forgot my keys. I won't be a moment."

He disappeared back into his office and was gone for several minutes before he returned. "Sorry. I couldn't find them at first. If you would follow me."

———

Beneath Museo Gregoriano Egiziano
Vatican City, Italy

Kane moaned, trying to move his arms towards his head to rid it of the shooting pain. The chains snapped taut, causing him to moan again.

"About time you woke up, you bastard."

Kane lifted his head, attempting to stare through the haze which seemed to be affecting his vision. He blinked a couple of times, but the gloom wouldn't clear. The voice came again, "Over here, Reaper."

"Cara?"

"Yes, it's me."

"I'm dreaming," Kane muttered.

"If you are, cobber, then so am I."

"Bluey?"

"Kinda takes him a while to get his head around things, doesn't it," the Australian said.

"Always was a little bit slow. Typical Jarhead."

"Who are you calling a Jarhead?"

"There he is," Cara said. "You got a plan?"

"I think the first part of it worked well," Bluey said. "At least we found you."

"Your friend is funny, Reaper," Cara said drily. "Seems like a lifetime ago since Somalia."

"What happened?" Kane asked.

"We got slugged from behind. I think the professor wasn't who he seemed to be," Bluey explained.

Kane winced and said, "You think?"

"Well, look on the bright side. We found who we were looking for. On both counts."

"That's the bright side?"

"It is if your name isn't Cara."

"Thanks for reminding me," Cara said.

Kane shook his head to rid himself of the last few cobwebs which remained. "Are you OK?" he asked her.

"I've been better. Is the team here?"

"Pretty much. All except Brick. He took a round in Pripyat. He's laid up in a hospital. Damn near lost him."

"Is he going to be OK?"

"I guess. He's in the right hands, anyway."

Movement deep in the catacombs revealed two men who came forward. Both of whom they knew; the professor and Craig Fletcher.

"Well, screw me over a rainbow," Bluey swore. "Just when you think you know someone."

"Do we ever really know someone?" Fletcher asked.

"Well, shit, obviously not."

"So, you're part of this too, professor?" Kane observed.

Bianchi nodded. "It would seem that way."

"What's next?" Kane asked.

"Tomorrow, we will complete the sacrificial rituals, and the Chosen One will kill the pope."

"The Chosen One?"

"That would be me," Fletcher said.

There was a moment of silence before Kane asked, "What happens to us?"

"You will watch the ritual, and then you will be killed, too."

"That's nice," Bluey said. "At least we get to watch the show before we check out. Do we get chips and Coke?"

Bianchi chuckled. "You are funny."

"Find out how funny I can be when I kill you."

The professor dismissed the comment with a wave of his hand and said, "I'm tired of this. We will return tomorrow when it is time."

Once they had disappeared back into the chamber, Cara turned to Kane and asked, "You got a plan?"

"Not yet."

"You working on one?"

"Kind of."

"Well, once you work it out, let me know."

"I'll do that."

———

Safehouse, Rome

"Do we have anything yet?" Thurston asked Ferrero.

"No, Ma'am, it's like they've just disappeared."

"Damn it. Find them. Get me Axe and Traynor. Carlos will stay here with you."

A few moments later, the two men were standing in front of their commander. "Listen up. Reaper and Bluey have disappeared. We know the location of where they were last, but that's it. They went to the museum and haven't been heard of since."

"So, they've been gone all night, Ma'am?" Axe asked.

"That's right."

"What do you want us to do?"

"Pete and I are headed over to the museum. Axe you head over to St. Peter's Square. The pope will be holding his mass outside the Basilica. Keep a look out for anything out of the ordinary."

"Cool. Me and Mike just hanging out."

Thurston glared at him.

"Or not. Weapons, Ma'am?" Axe asked.

"No."

"OK."

"I mean it," Thurston snapped.

"Yes, Ma'am."

"Get your comms organized. We leave in ten."

The general's next stop was Swift, who was busy trawling through security camera footage. "Do you have anything?"

"I have them going into the museum, and that's it. After that, nothing."

"They can't have just vanished."

"One would think not, but it would appear that they have."

"What about the cameras inside?"

"I can't access them. They're a closed circuit. I would need to be inside."

Thurston sighed. "That's not going to happen. Shit."

"I do have something else."

"Tell me."

Swift hit a couple of keys on his keyboard, and a picture came up. "This is Professor Bianchi leaving the museum yesterday afternoon."

"Who is that with him?"

"Craig Fletcher."

"Bluey's friend?"

"Yes."

"Is there any link between them that we don't know about?"

"None that I can find. Other than the fact that he goes to the museum at least twice a week."

"Keep working on it. There has to be a reason for him to be going there as often as that. See if you can match up any of his visits with the deaths of the women."

"Will do, Ma'am."

"I'll be on comms if you need me."

———

The crowd was starting to build in St. Peter's Square. Axe figured there was already at least ten thousand people in attendance. But that was just a fraction of the three-hundred-thousand it could hold. However, the crowd would build over the next few hours to a little more than half that number.

Axe walked past the Ancient Egyptian Obelisk and walked towards the Basilica. With a practiced eye, he looked around, taking in the security measures that were already in place. There were at least four snipers on the surrounding structures and any number of other armed men standing in the shadows.

The big ex-recon marine sniper reached the steps where it was roped off, and a podium had been placed behind bulletproof glass from which Pope Michael would make his speech. To his right stood a police officer who was watching over the perimeter. Axe walked over to him. "Hey, Buddy. Where can I find the Pope?"

The man stared at him, blankly and said, "*Chiedo scusa?*"

"You speak English?"

"*Scusa?*"

"I'll take that as a no," Axe said, rubbing at his beard. Then, "Pope Michael? In there?"

The man's eyes widened. "*Si, si.*"

Axe made to climb the rope only to be stopped by a firm hand pressing him hard in the chest. "*Fermati, non puoi andare lì dentro.*"

"I guess that means I can't go no further, huh?"

The stern expression said it all. Axe raised his hands in a conciliatory gesture and nodded. "OK, I'll go."

He turned away from the rope and walked back the way he'd come until he was directly beside the obelisk. From there, he looked at his surroundings until he found what he wanted. A way in. Now all he had to do was breach the perimeter to exploit it.

CHAPTER 19

Museo Gregoriano Egiziano
   Vatican City, Italy

Thurston and Traynor sat on a stone seat outside the museum, watching crowds of people coming and going, while they waited patiently for Swift to relay them some information. The computer tech was searching diligently for the schematics of the museum and where the professor kept his office. Their goal was to infiltrate quietly and question the man without causing too much fuss.

Suddenly his voice burst over their comms. "Bravo? Bravo Four, over."

Both Thurston and Traynor were dressed in casual clothes. Traynor in jeans and a collared shirt, while Thurston wore jeans and a white T-shirt with her hair tied back in a ponytail. They winced in reaction to the loud voice in their earpieces. "Copy, Bravo Four. Maybe keep it down a bit?"

"Sorry, Ma'am. But according to what I was able to find

out, the professor's office is in the back of the museum. I'll have to talk you through it."

"Fine."

"There is one more thing. I got a ping from facial rec, and Bluey's friend was back there."

"Seems like too much of a coincidence," Thurston said.

Traynor said, "I think we need to find these guys and now."

"I said was. He left thirty minutes ago."

"On his own?"

"Yes."

"OK, then, let's go."

"But wait, there's more," Swift said in a quiz-show kind of tone.

The general sighed. "Today is good."

"I don't know how it was missed, but I checked over the autopsy reports for the dead girls –"

"You what?" came the reply, cutting him off.

"Checked the autopsy records from the medical examiner."

"You know how to read those things?"

"In a fashion. Anyway, the more recent bodies had traces of a certain type of fungus on them. When I checked on it, I found out that it only grows in dark places below ground."

"So, they were killed underground?" Thurston asked.

"It would seem that way, Ma'am."

"Where around here would they be able to do that?"

"Rome is an ancient place, Ma'am," Swift said. "It has catacombs beneath it everywhere."

"What about here in Vatican City? The museum?"

"Possibly. I can see if I can find out."

"Do it while you're guiding us to the office of the professor."

"Yes, Ma'am."

––––––

Beneath Museo Gregoriano Egiziano
Vatican City, Italy

Bianchi stood beside Brother Red. He said, "It will soon be time. Get her ready."

Brother Red nodded. "Will you be doing it yourself, My Lord?"

"Yes."

"As you wish."

In the background, Brother White lurked in the shadows. Cara watched him and couldn't help but think how much she would like to cut his balls off before they killed her. Red moved toward her, a syringe appearing in his hand from the sleeve of his robe. Before she knew what was happening, he'd injected her with something.

Immediately, Cara's vision blurred, and her head slumped forward.

"Motherfucker!" Kane exclaimed. "What did you do?"

"She is only asleep. But just long enough to get her prepared on the sacrificial altar. They are a lot easier to handle that way."

Kane wrenched on his chains, and they snapped tautly. "You're dead, asshole."

Two other brothers emerged from the darkness and took Cara down. They carried her away, feet dragging on the damp cobbles. Bianchi said with a mirthless smile, "Enjoy the screams."

He followed in the others' wake, leaving the two men chained and feeling impotent. "I must say, he's a nice bloke," Bluey said sarcastically.

"Be even nicer with a bullet in his head," Kane responded caustically.

"So, what's the plan?"

"That is the million-dollar question."

———

Museo Gregoriano Egiziano
Vatican City, Italy

"Slick, he's not in his office," Thurston said into her comms. "What else do you have?"

"Sorry, Ma'am. Wait one."

"Don't take too long."

Traynor looked around the interior of the professor's office, and his gaze landed on the dark-stained bookcase. He walked over to it and studied the spines, his eyes alighting on one which stood out from the rest. The writing on the damaged spine was so faded it was barely legible, which told him that the book was well used. He slid it out and studied the title.

"Ma'am, I might have something here," Traynor said and opened it.

Thurston came to his side. "What is it?"

"It's a book on druids and shit like that. It's well used. More than any other book on the shelf."

He flicked through the ancient pages and stopped at a

hand-drawn picture. It was of a woman on an altar with a hooded man standing over her with a knife. Thurstone said, "That looks nice."

The ex-DEA man pointed to the caption beneath the picture which read, "It was believed that the power from all sacrifices would go to the Chosen One before battle." He read on and then said, "Here, General. This part says that the druids often sacrificed many people leading up to battles with their enemies."

"He's got to be our guy. Slick, do you have anything yet?"

"Ma'am, according to old maps I've found, there are a series of catacombs below the museum."

"How do we get down there?"

"Allow me."

––––––––

The Basilica

The only way to describe what he saw was magnificent. All of it. From the terrazzo floor to the gold gilding on the walls, and the stunning artwork to the marble statues. Axe shook his head in wonderment. "Man, this is some fucking ... oops, sorry, God. But man, you have some kind of house here."

"And he welcomes all who enter."

Axe turned towards the voice. Before him stood an elderly man dressed in off-white, and wearing a white zucchetto and a plain chain and crucifix. Recognition flooded Axe's face. "Mikey, that you?"

The elderly man smiled. "Not the place I would expect to find you, Axel."

"I guess we've both come up in the world."

"It is a long way from Angola."

That was where the pair had met. Axe had been part of a two-man sniper team inserted in country to perform a job against a local warlord who had been inciting violence against the Christian community. Things hadn't gone to plan when Axe's spotter was wounded, and he'd been forced to hide out at the mission where Father Michael had been serving at that time.

"Are you still doing God's work, Axel?" the Pope asked.

"Yes, sir. Still kicking the shi – ahh, still fighting on the side of the righteous."

"Good for you. Now, what brings you here?"

There was movement to the left, and a couple of security men appeared. They looked perplexed at the sight of the big ex-marine and started forward in a hurry. Pope Michael held up his hand and uttered something in Italian that Axe couldn't understand. The two men backed away hesitantly but not out of sight.

"Now, Axel, where were we?"

Axe said, "You're in trouble, Mikey. My team believes that someone is going to try to kill you."

Pope Michael's expression never changed. "Why do you think this?"

Axe went through everything pertinent as fast as he could without going into too much detail. When he was finished, the elderly man nodded. "What do you propose I should do about it?"

"I don't know, Mikey. Maybe cancel the blasted thing."

"I can't do that."

"So, you're going to stand up there and hope to Christ you don't get a bullet in your head?"

Pope Michael stared at him.

"Shit, sorry."

"I see your tongue is still as sharp as ever, Axel."

"I'm trying to keep you alive, Mikey."

"God will do that, Axel. If he decides to call me home, then so be it."

Axe sighed. "You're still as frustrating as ever."

"I could say the same about you."

"Do you mind if I take a look around to see if I can find anything?"

The Pope nodded. "I will tell my security that you should be accommodated and to give you whatever you ask for."

He waved at one of the men who came forward. The Pope spoke briefly, and the man frowned at him. The elderly man made a hurry up motion with his hand, and the security man reached inside his coat and took out a handgun. Pope Michael handed it across to Axe who gave him a questioning glance. The Pope placed a hand on his arm then said to him, "It's not the same world today as it was yesterday, Axel. Go with God." He made the sign of the cross.

"Don't forget to duck, Father."

"I'll try to remember."

————

St. Peter's Square,
Vatican City

"Slick, you're a smart man, aren't you?" Axe asked

There was a moment's hesitation before Swift came back with, "Why?"

"I need your help to figure out where this bastard is, and how he's going to kill Mikey."

"Who's Mikey?"

"The Pope, damn it."

"OK. What do you need?"

"I figure he will be a sniper. But the thing is the bullet-proof glass that will be in front. So, he either needs a clear line of sight, or there will be two shooters."

"Why two?"

"I figure maybe an armor-piercing round first up then a normal .308 follow up to take down the target."

"Why not a bomb?"

"Aw shit, don't throw that at me. That's something that I don't even want to consider. Is the boss there?"

"I'll get him."

While he waited, Axe paced, scanning all the places he figured he would set up a hide. A few moments later, Ferrero came on, "What's up, Reaper Four?"

"Boss, I've been given free rein to snoop around for any threats."

"Who gave you that?"

"Mikey."

"Who is Mikey?"

"The Pope."

"You're shitting me?"

"No, I ain't. I'll explain later." Axe continued pacing as he went on. "I told Slick we needed eyes in the air. What would really help is a satellite."

"I'll see what I can do."

"Any news from the general?"

No. They've gone underground."

"OK. I'll stay in touch."

"Be careful."

Axe scanned the square once more, letting his eyes roam over every surface and possible location, and then he saw it. Atop the Apostolic Palace. He was almost certain that the sniper who had been there wore a helmet. Now there were two there, and they both wore caps.

"Bravo Four, Copy?"

"Copy."

"Can you see two POIs on top of the Apostolic Palace?"

"Wait one."

It was then that Axe realized that the crowd had swelled exponentially. They were jammed into the front half of the square. A few moments later, Swift said, "I can't get a clear view of them, Reaper Four."

Suddenly the crowd began to cheer. Axe looked about and saw that the Pope had appeared on the steps of the Basilica and was making his way to the podium. "Shit! It's too late, Slick. Mikey's just come out. I'm going for the roof."

———

Beneath Museo Gregoriano Egiziano
Vatican City, Italy

Thurston and Traynor moved stealthily along the dimly lit corridor on rubber-soled boots. Movement up ahead made them step back into the inky blackness of the shadows. Somewhere, from further away in the direction they were heading, came the sound of low chanting. Thurston touched Traynor on the shoulder, and he slipped out of the shadow and moved forward once more.

They had found the entrance to the catacombs

concealed behind a large wall tapestry. From there, a stone staircase wound down into the damp depths of the unknown.

The faint glow of firelight flickered along the stone block walls, causing the shadows to dance. As they closed the distance, the chanting grew louder. Being careful so as not to be seen, Traynor peered tentatively around the corner of the stone wall and into the lit chamber where he saw five men, four of whom were dressed in white robes. The fifth one was wearing a garment of bright blue. His arms were upright, and the dancing light from the blazing torch wall-sconces caught the long blade of the knife he held aloft.

"Hold it right there, asshole!"

Moving into the chamber, Traynor's voice echoed throughout the small space, causing them to turn in his direction. Beside him, Thurston said, "Get the knife."

Realizing what she'd said, Bianchi tried to bring the knife down in between Cara's exposed breasts.

Traynor moved quickly, and his right hand clamped down on the blade, the sharp edge cutting deep to the bone. He bit back a curse of pain but didn't let go. Instead, he focused his gaze on the professor, and his left fist looped over and landed flush on the man's jaw.

"Take that, you crazy fucker," he uttered through clenched teeth.

Bianchi cried out and fell backward, disappearing behind the altar. Thurston appeared beside the ex-DEA man and shoved the dumbstruck cloaked men out of the way. A snarl from one of them drew her attention as Brother White launched himself at her.

With practiced ease, she brought her right elbow around and smashed it into the center of the man's bruised face. With a sickening crunch, his broken nose mashed into his sinus cavity and up into his brain, and he collapsed at Thurston's feet. She checked Cara who was still out cold and then turned to look at the others. "Are you pricks going to cause us any more trouble?"

Two of them stepped back, leaving one standing close to the altar. "Who are you?"

"I am no one," Brother Red said.

"Where are my men?"

He said nothing, but his eyes flickered and gave it away. Thurston looked at Traynor and noticed his hand. "Are you OK?"

"Nothing a couple of dozen stitches won't fix."

"Shit. Hang in there and keep an eye on these assholes. I'll be back."

Walking around the altar, she grabbed Brother Red roughly and shoved him ahead of her. "Move."

She found her team members in chains where they'd been left. When Kane saw his boss, he said, "Boy, am I glad to see you. Did you find Cara? How is she?"

"She's OK," the general answered as she turned the druid around so she could watch him. "Give me the key to the manacles!"

"I don't have it," the man answered evenly.

"Bullshit," spat Kane. "You locked us in here."

The general moved in close to Brother Red and grabbed him by the throat. "Give me the fucking key! I don't have time for this shit."

The man reached into his robe and produced a key on a leather string. He handed to the general, and she released him, giving him a shove for good measure.

Moving across to Reaper, she began to free them.

While the general worked on Bluey's restraints, Kane

rubbed his wrists briskly then stepped forward and punched the druid in the mouth. He spat on the floor and said, "Fuck you."

"Feel better?"

"Much," Kane said. "We have to get topside. They're going to kill the Pope."

"I've got Axe on it as we speak. We pieced it together. Right now, though, we need to secure these guys and get Pete to a medic."

———

Apostolic Palace

When Axe reached the roof of the palace, there were no thoughts of creeping up on those who were there. Time had run out, and he needed to stop whoever it was before they were able to enact their plan.

The handgun, a Beretta 92FS, swept up as he made his way along the rooftop. He found them soon after, one hunched over a sniper rifle, his companion beside him with another weapon. Axe's theory had been right. He'd come up behind them, so both were looking in the opposite direction.

On the roof beside them was the prone figure of the dead police sniper who'd originally been placed there. The ex-marine's jaw set firm, then. "Hey, assholes."

The sniper on the left turned his head, surprised to see Axe standing there holding a gun. The second man, however, didn't move. He was now the primary threat. Axe's weapon aimed to the right and fired twice. The bullet from the Beretta punched into the back of the man's head, knocking him forward. The shooter's trigger finger curled reflexively, and the rifle roared.

The bullet flew harmlessly skyward which was lucky

considering the extensive number of civilians in the square below. The remaining shooter reacted immediately and rolled to his left, trying to bring the heavy, large caliber rifle in his hands to bear. It was a slow, cumbersome move and Axe had all the time in the world to put a bullet in the sniper's head. With the Beretta still raised, Axe moved forward to check the fallen men.

A round whistled as it tore through the air directly at Axe, although it didn't register in his mind what it was before the hammer blow knocked him back. All the air rushed from his lungs, and he tried helplessly to draw in more. His mouth opened and closed until he finally managed to inflate them.

The ex-marine tried to rise, but everything was numb. He felt the wetness and touched it with his hand. Then Axe brought it up in front of his face. His hand was covered in blood.

"Fuck me, I've been shot," he mumbled. "The bastards shot me."

"Zero? Man down. Zero – Zer –"

And everything went black.

―――

Museo Gregoriano Egiziano
Vatican City, Italy

"Axe is down! I repeat, Axe is down, he's been shot! There's another shooter."

"Shit!" Thurston hissed. "Reaper, Axe is down."

"Christ, where?"

Traynor reached up and took his earpiece out. "Here, Reaper, take this. Go."

Kane had been helping Cara who looked at him, her eyes still a little hazy from the drugs. "Go, Reaper."

"I'll come with you," Bluey said.

Thurston gave him her comms and watched them head off at a sprint. In a low voice, she said, "Good luck."

There was chaos out in the square. A crush of humanity moved like a giant wave as their panic rose to a fever pitch. Kane said, "This is not good."

Bluey nodded. "You go to your man. I'll look for the shooter. I've a feeling I know who it is and where he's going."

"Roger that."

The two men separated, Kane running towards the palace. "What do you have for me, Slick?"

"Medics are on their way, Reaper. There are already security personnel on the rooftop with him."

"Fine. Now help Bluey find that fucking shooter."

"I can't. You've seen what it's like down there."

"Try, damn it."

"Yes, sir."

When Kane broke out onto the rooftop, three armed men who were standing over Axe, turned their weapons to face the new arrival, while a fourth continued to work on the fallen man. Kane threw his arms in the air and shouted to the men that he was a friendly and not to shoot. The men didn't comprehend his words, but his hand actions indicated that he was with Axe and they hesitantly lowered their weapons.

When he reached Axe's side, he knelt beside his friend, looking down at all the blood that was on the roof surface, and the man's pallid complexion told him that this could only be a fatal injury. It was at that point that he picked up Axe's hand and said goodbye to his friend.

———

The Basilica

Bluey ran up the steps of the Basilica and found his first body just inside the main entrance. The security man had taken a bullet to his chest and lay in a pool of blood. The Australian reached down and picked up the Beretta which had been dropped and checked the loads. It was good.

He heard the voices before he entered the cathedral. Just outside were two more of the Pope's security detail. Bluey said into his comms, "I have three down in the Basilica, and I'm pretty sure our guy is in here with the Pope. I'm going to take a look."

"Stand down, Bluey," Ferrero ordered.

"If I do that, the Pope is as good as dead. Bluey, out."

With the Beretta raised, he walked into the cathedral and immediately saw Fletcher standing with the Pope in the nave about a third of the way to the papal altar. The Brit had a handgun pointed at the Pope who was trying to reason with his executioner.

Bluey said, "Fletch, now would be a good time to put the gun down, Mate. It's all over."

"It is not over until I kill the heathen Pope."

"Why? I've not heard any of you idiots say why."

His eyes grew crazy, and he said, "Because our Gods will it, that's why."

Bluey shook his head and said, "Batshit crazy."

He squeezed the trigger on the gun, and the bullet

punched into the head of his one-time friend. Fletcher dropped like a stone to the solid floor. Out of habit, Bluey moved in quickly and kicked the weapon away from the dead man. He looked at the stunned Pope and asked, "Are you OK, Cobber?"

Pope Michael nodded dumbly.

"I'm sorry about that, Father. I had to do it, or he would have killed you."

"God will forgive you, my son."

"I'm not so sure about that," Bluey told him. Then into his comms, he said, "The package is secure."

EPILOGUE

Rome, Italy
Four Days Later

Axe coughed once before opening his eyes. At first, his vision was blurred, and then as it cleared, a face swam into view. He tried to speak but nothing was forthcoming. Swallowing to moisten his dry throat, it felt like coarse sandpaper had been used on it. He said, "Are we both dead?"

Cara smiled. "You think I would hang out with you if we were both dead?"

"I feel like I should be."

"You very nearly were," Kane said to him from the other side of the bed.

Axe turned his head and grinned at him. "Hey, amigo, now I know I ain't dead. If I was, you sure as shit wouldn't be here. I'd be surrounded by lots of pretty women just like Cara and the general."

"Are you talking about me?" Thurston asked.

Alarm suddenly registered on his face. "Permission to die, Ma'am?"

"Not yet, Axel. I have things planned for you."

"Damn it, Reaper, she called me Axel."

"She did."

"Did we get the bad guys?"

"Yes."

"How's Mikey?"

Kane frowned. "Mikey?"

"The Pope."

Thurston frowned and said, "About that. You actually know Pope Michael?"

"Sure. He's a nice guy. We go way back. Is he OK?"

"Thanks to Bluey."

The Australian stepped forward. "How are you feeling, Cobber?"

"Axe glared at him and then asked Kane, "Did he just cuss at me?"

With a chuckle, Kane shook his head. "No, you dumb ox."

Thurston patted Axe on the arm. "We'll get out of here and let you get some rest."

"You're leaving me on my own?"

"No, Cara is in the bed beside you, and Traynor is down the hall."

"Pete?"

"Yes, he got his hand cut up."

"OK."

"We'll be back tomorrow. You two get some rest."

As they walked out of the room door, Kane heard Axe say to Cara, "Did I tell you about the time I was on Guam?"

To which she replied, "Shut up, Axe."

"Sounds like they'll get along fine," Bluey said, laughing.

"Yeah, I have a good team. What about you? Where are you off to?"

"We're all back to Afghanistan. Unfinished business."

Kane nodded and held out his hand. "Good luck, Bluey. And thanks for all of your help."

"It's been fun. Keep your head down."

"You too."

———

Sangin Valley
Afghanistan

The breaching charge blew, and a pall of dust exploded from the mud walls surrounding it. The sound of grenades exploding the distance reached Bluey's ears. Beside him, he heard Jacko call, "Frag out!" and he leaned forward and threw the grenade into the opened hole.

With a CRUMP, the thing exploded, and the men of Bluey's team went in after their target. Movement to Bluey's right drew his attention, and a short burst from his M4 put the insurgent down. Behind him, he sensed rather than saw Ringa. He went left and cleared the room there.

They worked their way methodically through the compound until almost every part of it was clear, leaving just one more room.

With a mighty crash, the door slammed back on its hinges, and Bluey was first in through the dark opening. He swept the room briefly before firing off a short burst, which was followed by the words, "Got the bastard."

When he re-emerged from the dimly lit room, he looked relieved and triumphant. Pressing his transmit button, he spoke the words he'd been itching to say. "This is Bushranger One to all channels. Ned Kelly is down, I say again, Ned Kelly is down. Secure the perimeter and prepare for exfil."

A LOOK AT: LETHAL TENDER
(TEAM REAPER BOOK 7)

BY BRIAN DRAKE

John Kane might be on a mission, but he's experiencing a crisis of confidence this time around...

A jailed cartel leader buried a fortune—and it's a kill or be killed race to find it!

Caesario Crisfulli is a major player in the French-Italian Corridor, the biggest drug syndicate in Europe. Crisfulli needs the cash to fund a mercenary army for his plans to dethrone the syndicate leader and take over. He's motivated not by greed, but by revenge...

John Kane and Team Reaper have put the destruction of the French-Italian Corridor on the top of their priority list. If Crisfulli thinks he can simply dig up the money and control the flow of drugs through Europe, he has another thing coming.

The seventh book in the adrenalin-pumping Team Reaper series is guaranteed to keep you glued to your seat!

AVAILABLE NOW

ABOUT THE AUTHOR

A relative newcomer to the world of writing, Brent Towns self-published his first book, a western, in 2015. *Last Stand in Sanctuary* took him two years to write. His first hardcover book, a Black Horse Western, was published the following year. Since then, he has written a further 26 western stories, including some in collaboration with British western author, Ben Bridges.

Also, he has written the novelization to the upcoming 2019 movie from One-Eyed Horse Productions, titled, Bill Tilghman and the Outlaws. Not bad for an Australian author, he thinks.

He says, "The obvious next step for me was to venture into the world of men's action/adventure/thriller stories. Thus, Team Reaper was born."

A country town in Queensland, Australia, is where Brent lives with his wife and son.

For more information:
https://wolfpackpublishing.com/brent-towns/

Made in the USA
Las Vegas, NV
20 February 2023

67830914R00157